RENEWALS 458-4574
DATE DUE

GAYLORD

PRINTED IN U.S.A.

The Glass Slipper
and Other Stories

Originally published in Japanese as "Garasu no kutsu," "Shukudai," "Ginyu shijin,"
"Hausu gardo," "Jinguru beru," "Ohsama no mimi," "Kenbu," "Kunsho," and
"Tsukiji odawara-cho" by Kodansha

Library of Congress Cataloging-in-Publication Data

Yasuoka, Shotaro, 1920-
The glass slipper and other stories / Shotaro Yasuoka ; translation
by Royall Tyler.
p. cm.
Translation of "Garasu no kutsu" and eight other works selected by
the Japanese Literature Publishing Project (JLPP).
ISBN-13: 978-1-56478-504-6 (alk. paper)
ISBN-10: 1-56478-504-1 (alk. paper)
1. Yasuoka, Shotaro, 1920---Translations into English. I. Tyler,
Royall. II. Title.
PL865.A7A6 2008
895.6'35--dc22
                    2007045756

This book has been selected by the Japanese Literature Publishing Project (JLPP),
which is run by the Japanese Literature Publishing and Promotion Center (J-Lit
Center) on behalf of the Agency for Cultural Affairs of Japan

Partially funded by a grant from the Illinois Arts Council, a state agency, and by
the University of Illinois, Urbana-Champaign

cover art: "Takasaki Station" © Yoko Kawazoe
www.dalkeyarchive.com
Printed on permanent/durable acid-free, recycled paper
and bound in the United States of America

The Glass Slipper and Other Stories

Shotaro Yasuoka

Translated from the Japanese by Royall Tyler

Dalkey Archive Press
Champaign and London

Stories

The Wandering Minstrel

This year on New Year's Day I had a dream. The morbidly unpleasant impression it left suggests that it may ultimately have set me on the path toward the present impossible situation to which my own foolishness has led me.

I was pushing a baby carriage into a pasture dotted with gray cows. Suddenly I felt warmth on my back and realized it was because I was carrying another baby there. I was taking my children to be nursed. The pasture somehow resembled a Spanish bullfighting ring, large and sturdily fenced, and around it stood a crowd of men dressed just like me. In age they seemed to run from about thirty—my own age—to fifty or so. With baby drool running down the backs of their necks, they were all clutching their *nenneko* coats—the kind that is meant to cover the baby, too—around them and holding, each and every one of them, a bottle of milk.

"I just don't know what to do!" all were saying to one another. "*Mine* gives me only half of what's in her pay envelope."

"Yours isn't the only one, you know!"

It was their wives they were all gossiping about—how they were at work, what they were like. Then I recognized, among all these men wearing *nenneko* coats over their babies, some of the bright students and diligent grinds I'd known in my school days. These superior characters looked just like all the others. There was nothing different about them, but in my dream I envied and resented their especially shiny bottles. That these men, genuine men, should have no need to go to work, that it should be their main task each day simply to take their babies to the pasture to be fed, and that afterwards they should have nothing to do but lie around on the grass, staring up at the clouds and waiting for their wives to come home from the government offices where they were employed—the more I digested all this, the more I was overcome by an odd mixture of lassitude and relief, and, even sound asleep, sank into an ever more engulfing stupor.

They say it's scientifically possible to determine a person's desires and personality by analyzing the person's dreams, but I wonder. Surely women have always been more fanciful creatures than men, more given to the pursuit of practical abstractions. That's my opinion, anyway. I'm not married. I've been in love a few times, but it never went very far, and on that score I feel as though failure is probably my fate.

I couldn't very well spend the first three days of the New Year just lying around in that room of mine, drafty as a birdcage, out beyond the fringes of the city, so each day I set off to visit this or that house. Actually, making the rounds of the houses of people I knew had no particular connection with New Year's. For years I'd been spending at least half of every month dining in other people's houses, and that mode of life perfectly suited the season. No doubt I was just like that, anyway. To tell the truth, I was very good at cadging meals off others. Even in childhood I'd found exactly the same dish tastier when eaten in someone else's house, and when I grew up I learned to make a fine show of rapture over absolutely anything I was served. That skill now stood me in good stead financially. Of course, I knew perfectly well what a deplorable character I was, but only in an intellectual, theoretical way. In my heart of hearts I didn't give it a second thought. Besides, my technique in the matter was my only accomplishment. Four or five years earlier I'd floundered my way to graduation from a private university, but since then I'd gotten by without ever managing to find a decent job. It was New Year's, and the saké flowed practically everywhere I went. Apart from that, I might have had a cold coming on, because on the morning of January fourth, done in from too much food and drink, I had the unpleasant feeling when I left for the company where I worked that my brains and stomach were all mixed up with each other. What awaited me that day was quite a surprise.

I call the place a company, but really it was just a small knitwear wholesale outfit with ten employees, located in a corner of the textile wholesale district of Nihonbashi. I'd been on temporary contract there since the previous autumn, with the title of "translator." This involved quite a contrast. There I was, at the very back of a shop open to every breeze and piled high with *tabi* socks, *koshimaki* belly bands, *patchi* work pants, and so on, poring over Western fashion magazines full of articles about trends in furs and jewelry. The shop and I were at odds with each other, no doubt about it. With my scanty ability at languages, I struggled as well as I could to make sense of what was printed there on the glossy art paper, but nothing of all my labor served the company in any way.

After racking my brains for hours over the dictionary, I'd finally manage to copy down on my writing pad, as though I knew what I was doing, something like, for example, "Over a period of ___ weeks in ___ of 195_, a retail store in Antwerp sold seventy dozen pairs of women's work pants. This unusual situation bears watching." The whole thing was an idiotic waste of time, but no, I didn't quit. Why?

Because I didn't know how to do anything else. I couldn't handle an abacus, and I'd have been hopeless as a shipping clerk. Why had they ever hired someone like me in the first place? Because the owner, Sugimoto Shigezô, made a hobby of composing poems—not those classical poems in thirty-one syllables, but something more like folk songs or army song lyrics, completely free in meter and so on. That was Mr. Sugimoto's great pleasure, and as it happened, I'd once hummed a song that he really liked. He adopted it as the Sugimoto Knitwear Company song and, at the same time, took me on as a temporary worker there.

The company song parodied the *chii chii pappa* of the children's song by turning it into *don don pappa*. It went:

> *don don pappa*
> *don pappa*
> our knitwear from
> good old Japan . . .

It didn't sound like much when I sang it, but when sung by Mr. Sugimoto, the company president, the *don don pappa* came booming out with stirring power. Having left a poverty-stricken village in Iwate Prefecture of northern Japan to arrive penniless in Tokyo and build up this business of his all on his own, Mr. Sugimoto was cautiously, even pusillanimously frugal in his ways, but he loved doing things in a grand manner as long as there was no money involved. Every morning, in the coldest weather, he'd stand everyone out in the street in front of the shop for the morning gathering, which included singing *don don pappa*. As a result the songwriter, namely me, was cordially detested by every one of his employees. In any case, they had ample reason to regard me as "the boss's toady," besides which I was so utterly useless—I couldn't even write an address on an address label properly—that in their eyes I was simply a parasite whose salary was sheer thievery. "We can do very well, thank you, without translations from foreign magazines," the old-timers would remark loudly enough to be sure I heard, "and anyway, *that* clown's translations make no sense at all." No doubt they were right. As I sat there at my desk, impelled by an odd sense of duty, my efforts somehow to connect articles so remote from current Japanese reality with the underwear items my company sold, forced me to twist every mention of fur into something about cotton flannel. As a result, my posture in the company was that of a chicken in a gale: stock-still, head low, darting the odd glance around to keep an eye on the others, and doing all I could to stay out of everyone's way. That was my sole concern. The company's old-timers were by no means alone in giving me a hard time. A new office girl just out of high school would do the same thing, and Mr. Sugimoto, every bit as emotional as his passion for poetry suggests, would start roaring at me in that booming voice of his whenever, for some almost always unfathomable reason, he felt the least bit out of sorts.

On January fourth the company's clients were shut, so once our president had delivered his New Year greeting and passed out sushi box lunches with a pint of saké each, we, too, closed. Somehow it didn't feel right, though, for us all to just go on home, so instead we stood around the stove while Y, the chief clerk, poured us teacups of cold saké. I thought Mr. Sugimoto had left already when suddenly his voice summoned me from the back of the shop. "Hey, Fukada!" he called—that was my last name. "Fukada, get in here!" He often had a way of sneaking up on us when we least expected it, and we'd be overcome by the illusion that we were goofing off, even when we weren't at all. In fear and trembling I headed for the back room, wondering whether I'd completely forgotten some work I'd promised to do, or whether this was perhaps about the lyrics for the song "Hama-chô Boogie," which he'd told me to ghostwrite for him, but which I hadn't even started yet.

There the company president stood, still in his cutaway. He was short and roly-poly, and the skin of his short neck was pink where the white collar bit into it. He smiled when he saw me.

I smiled back, wondering for no particular reason whether I was about to be fired. My half-year contract would be up in February.

"Sit down," Mr. Sugimoto said, thrusting a cushion toward me. What he had in mind, though, was something far more improbable. He wanted to know whether I mightn't like to marry his niece.

I felt great. This was something that could change my world. The red-faced man sitting before me would suddenly be transformed into "Uncle." If that's not astonishing magic, what is?

At twenty-eight she was three years younger than me. She'd graduated from a women's vocational school. Her health was sound, and her parents', too. Listening to all this with half an ear, I devoted most of my energy to chasing down my turbulent feelings.

"On the other hand," he continued, "*your* health isn't that strong, and you're too much of an easygoing romantic to succeed in business."

My astonishment grew. His simple way of telling the unvarnished truth flustered me as much as if he'd tugged at my underwear. Yes, I was an easygoing romantic.

"So a man like you needs a dependable wife who's a good earner."

"Right, right."

"Fortunately, her father's given her an established knitwear shop that should do to support both of you."

When Mr. Sugimoto spoke I normally just chimed in to agree, no matter what he said, but I was in no hurry to do the same this time. Quite apart from my surprise, indeed my amazement, I felt as though the blood circulating through this body of mine—a body already thrown into chaos by overeating and drinking too much ever since New Year's Day—had suddenly gone into reverse.

The prospective couple's formal introduction to each other was to take place the following day, January fifth, at a dinner to which I was invited at the young lady's house. This invitation prompted me to ask a question that really concerned me.

"Is the young lady's face round, or is it oval?"

I'd always assumed that most good-looking girls had oval faces, but that that shape also left room for unpleasant oddities, whereas round faces were more predictable and so, on balance, somewhat safer.

"She has a round face," Mr. Sugimoto promptly replied.

Come to think of it, he was round-faced, too.

My mind plunged into renewed turmoil once I was alone again. Walking along without even noticing that I was walking, I arrived in no time at Nihonbashi Station. I'd already fallen into the state—that of the anxious lover—in which hope and despair alternate as fast as a cat's eye shifts. To tell the truth, I'd been through such a formal introduction to a woman once before, in the summer of the previous year, thanks to a friend from my student days, Isono Matsutarô. I'd hesitated at the time, for no particular reason, but Isono prevailed on me to go with him to the coffee shop where we were to wait. In the end, the woman chose Isono over me. That experience provoked a jealousy that was this time wholly imaginary. I just hope there's no other young man there tomorrow! I kept saying to myself. I remembered Mr. Sugimoto looking askance at my clothes, though, so I went to Isono's place to borrow some. He was the only friend who wore my size.

"What's up?" Isono asked, taking out a dark blue pin-striped double-breasted suit. "Another marriage introduction?"

"Oh no, nothing like that. It's just that I need it for a little while."

I wasn't embarrassed or anything. My reply sprang instead from a superstitious dread that the whole business would be ruined if I told him. Still, I couldn't keep a shame-faced smile from spreading over my face as I lied.

The next day I had no end of trouble just getting though the hours until evening. The normally short winter day seemed interminable. Looking in the mirror to shave made me somehow melancholy. An inexpressible gloom came over me when I went to iron my borrowed trousers or pondered whether to put a handkerchief in the breast pocket, and I recalled a phrase from somewhere: "Who are they all for, these colors I'm putting on?" By this time, I was even tormented by the suspicion that I might be slipping into some sort of perverted state of mind.

In the end I couldn't stand it anymore and left, despite being afraid I might be a little early. When I reached the company, though, I found Mr. Sugimoto already there in the back room, dressed for the occasion, waiting for me. I greeted him with a bow.

"Let's go," he said instantly.

"Yes, sir."

I followed my short company president to the main street, where we waited for a taxi. In the chill evening air Mr. Sugimoto gave off a mothball odor strong enough to sting my nose a little.

The young lady's house was across the river. I didn't recognize the route, never having been that way before, but through the taxi window I saw tall smokestacks thrusting up into the night sky. I suppose these are the times when you have premonitions, good or bad. I got the feeling I was making some sort of mistake. What gave me that feeling I couldn't tell, but I had a hunch that what was coming was not what I'd imagined.

The taxi stopped in front of a haberdashery, one so ordinary in appearance that I entered it without a qualm. In the sitting room at the back I was introduced to the young lady's parents. Putting my hands to the floor in a formal bow brought back to me the mood you experience before a judo bout; so that was all right, too. When the refreshments arrived, however, the evil premonition I'd had in the taxi became all too real. Each of us was served a wooden tray bearing cocoa and *monaka* wafers filled with bean jam. The *monaka* wafers were heaped on the dish almost to overflowing, and a massive bean jam filling oozed from between every wafer pair. Each one menaced me like a hand grenade. What on earth was I supposed to do with them? With that mountain before my eyes, I wavered; whereupon Mr. Sugimoto, from beside me, shot me a glance with that red face of his, as though commanding me to eat. I desperately forced them all down, my throat practically raw from the mingled sweetness of bean jam and chocolate, only to be dismayed yet again by what instantly appeared next: six hard-boiled eggs each and yet another mountain, this one of pickled Chinese cabbage. These were accompanied by a saké cup. This time, however, I pitched into the feast with a will, for a very good reason. I should have guessed it from the start, of course, but anyway, I'd suddenly realized that the person who'd been serving us all this from the beginning was the young lady herself. How could I possibly have missed it? Yes, her face was round, and she looked like both of her parents. Under the circumstances, I had no choice but to eat and drink. The business of washing down one hard-boiled egg after another with saké seems to have gotten me a bit drunk.

"Please have some more," the young lady said, placing the saké jar before me; at which silence descended on the room. Then it happened. The saké cup in my hand began to tremble. Thanks to some train of association, the young lady's broad, pale face looked like one of the cows I'd seen in my New Year's Day pastoral dream. It was at once ridiculous and terrifying.

I realized when I got back to my room that night that I was more than somewhat intoxicated. A feeling of indescribable desolation overwhelmed me. It was like disappointment in love, only worse. Why was I feeling this way? Was it because the girl had looked like a cow? Apart from being tall and heavy, she hadn't been in the least like a cow. At any rate, the moment I reached to accept the saké she offered to pour me, I lost all nervousness or embarrassment. I no longer feared Mr. Sugimoto, either, even though normally it frightened me to be near him. Instead, everything became as tasteless as sand.

Such was my mood that I awarded myself a four-day vacation on the grounds that it was still New Year's Week. On the fifth day, I showed my face at the company, wondering whether to cite a cold or a hangover as an excuse for not having turned up before, and I realized then and there that I was stuck with a painful predicament. Mr. Sugimoto called me into the back room as soon as he spotted me.

"The Kurahara family tell me they'd like very much to have another talk with you," he said.

In other words, they presumably wanted to decide the date of the wedding, etc. I could hardly believe it. For once I'd apparently been a great success.

"But . . ." I started to say, then fell silent. There was no way to explain that I didn't much care for the idea, and I certainly couldn't bring up the business of the cow. I fell back on asking him for two or three days off so I could go and inform my parents. With that, he and I parted.

Strange things happen. If they'd actually liked me, then I must have unconsciously deployed my sole talent, getting people to give me a good feed at their houses, and my appreciation of the *monaka* wafers and the hard-boiled eggs must have been really convincing. By the way, the news that they'd liked me brought to mind even more sharply the cow image I'd connected with the girl. At first, the memory of those cows had given me a feeling of bleak tedium, but then the very sight of a cow had begun to strike fear into me.

The three-day reprieve I'd gotten myself to think up a way out passed in a flash. If I stayed away from work any longer I'd well and truly be out of a job. I still couldn't say I didn't want to marry her, though. If I did, I'd have to answer to Mr. Sugimoto, who'd put so much effort into arranging the whole thing. Obviously I'd be fired, but I wasn't at all sure it would end there. The more I thought about it, the more I had to conclude that sheer survival required me to go and tell him I'd do it. At my wits' end, I finally came up with the following.

OK, every thought of the girl reminded me of a cow. Furthermore, I was so frightened of cows that I wasn't afraid of Mr. Sugimoto. So perhaps I could avoid losing my job if I spent my working hours thinking of absolutely nothing but the girl . . .

Anyway, I left my place determined to give it a try. I took the subway as usual to Nihonbashi and walked to the company from there. On the way I practiced keeping my mind on just that one thing. I turned up my overcoat collar, put my hand over my nose, and left just an opening for my eyes to see the way ahead. That way, I thought, I'd be able to maintain my concentration. The others around me were all heading to work, and not one of them seemed to find the way I walked at all odd.

At last I reached the corner of the company's street. This is it, I told myself, and I screwed my imagination up to the highest pitch of concentration. Apparently I was a little late, because the morning gathering was already under way. I'd just registered this when I heard a chorus of voices singing *don don pappa*. I froze.

> *don don pappa*
> *don pappa*
> our knitwear from
> good old Japan . . .

I'd written that song! In fact, I'd been living off it for a whole five months. Mr. Sugimoto's voice, rich and powerful, rang out above the rest, but I just couldn't go any nearer. The image I'd been cultivating with such fierce determination vanished as though scattered to the winds.

The Glass Slipper

Even Nihonbashi is quiet after midnight.

Now and again you catch the distant, ostentatious whine of a car engine speeding off down the expressway.

"What's up?"

I adjusted my grip on a receiver slippery with sweat, put my feet up on the table, and arched my back against the chair. It was Etsuko. She was in bed.

"See, I have this hankering to meet a bear. Did you ever see a bear make off with a fish?"

"Nope."

"Come on, you've got to try harder than that. Bears are great. They say bears can talk to people. You think that's true?"

"No idea."

"You claim you were born in Hokkaido, though. You really don't know?"

As Etsuko's voice came through the fine, vibrating steel membrane, I gazed at the row of blue-black hunting guns lined up behind the glass doors. Flat-chested, childlike Etsuko, with her gangly arms and legs—every time I held her tight, she felt as though she'd break against me. But when she took into her head to resist, she offered no hold anywhere—I might as well have been underwater, tangled in seaweed. What *is* this about bears? I murmured to myself. I was going to have to do something, and soon. But that was probably just what Etsuko had in mind. This business of wanting to meet a bear was some sort of signal to me.

"The summer vacation will be over soon, won't it. How many more days?"

"I don't want to talk about it!"

I'd purposely brought up a taboo subject between us.

Waiting was my job. I was employed as a night watchman in a store that sold hunting guns. I was supposed to be on guard all night against burglary and fire. It wasn't work. I was just like the hygrometer or the thermometer on the wall of the ammunition room. A thermometer is no good for detecting fire, and I didn't have it in me to put up a fight against an intruder. All I did was wait for fire and burglars to show up.

Their dismal failure to do so kept me employed. Being homeless otherwise, I could at least eat and keep a roof over my head at night. During the day I went to school, to sleep on a classroom chair.

The shop owner had me deliver a birding shotgun to the house of Lieutenant Colonel Craigow, a U.S. Army doctor who lived in Harajuku. This wasn't exactly part of my job description, besides which it was a warm day in early May, and I sneezed miserably all the way there. Still, I got a little welcome when I arrived. The pale, skinny maid brought me something to drink and nibble on. She smiled bashfully when she saw me, the way someone might do after letting out a fart. To me, she looked like a sheep. She somehow reminded me of a white sheep munching on paper. An aging black-and-white spotted pointer opened the kitchen door by itself and came wandering in. I held out a cracker to make it beg, but it ignored me. The dog refused to eat the cracker till the maid spread cheese on it. Finally it shot me a suspicious glance and plunked itself down at the maid's feet, like a scholar slumped, chin in hand, at his desk. In fits and starts she told me that Craigow and his wife were leaving the next day on a long trip to the island of Angaur, and that she was supposed to look after their house alone for the next three months. When I went to leave, she asked whether I wouldn't stay a little longer. I started to light my pipe, and she offered me a cigarette. There was a strange weakness to her gestures. When she struck a match for me, her awkward way of holding it by the very end made her seem to be afraid of the flame. Suddenly it occurred to me that she might well be a pampered young lady.

I ended up staying longer than I'd planned. When I left, she smiled that bashful smile again and asked me to come back once in a while, if I liked. I did just that. It was a lot better than going to the school, where there were only hard chairs.

That's how Etsuko and I became close. Still, I never imagined that I'd eventually fall in love with her. Honestly, she wasn't that attractive.

I went there one day a week later to find her wearing a *yukata* cotton kimono with a pattern of tennis rackets on it. She wasn't feeling well, she said. I teased her that the pattern looked childish, and we went on to talk about our summer vacations when we were in elementary school. Etsuko said she'd been a top student. Come to think of it, her pallid skin and her oddly proper appearance *did* have something of the class president. Still, she'd hated the start of school just like me, the perennial dunce. How sad they'd been, the dying days of the vacation, and how each of us, childishly lonely, had fretted our way through them amid the debilitating heat! It's not exactly that we missed the experience, or that anything about it seemed nostalgic.

We just understood each other on that score. I mentioned how awful it had felt to spend the day goofing off yet again and to stare at a mountain of untouched homework while, outside, the *higurashi* shrilled.

"Have you ever seen a *higurashi* bird?" she suddenly asked.

That got me. Etsuko was twenty years old. She smiled a vague little smile when I asked her to say that again.

"A *higurashi* isn't a bird," I explained. "It's an insect—a kind of cicada."

Etsuko could hardly believe it. "*Really*?" she said, round-eyed with wonder (she had beautiful eyes). "I thought it was a bird, a big one, like this." Her gesture suggested something the size of a watermelon. I was entranced. Before my eyes flashed visions of butterflies as big as donkeys, praying mantises the size of dogs, and so on. I was so tickled that I laughed out loud. She burst into tears.

"You're always making things up! I mean, I've *seen* one! At Karuizawa!"

She wept on my shoulder, the tears streaming down her cheeks. I hardly knew what to do.

"Hmm, well, perhaps there *are* some at Karuizawa. Actually, I've never seen a *higurashi* myself."

From beside her I put my arms around her, and we stayed like that for a while. Her wet and shining eyes looked bigger than ever. I gazed at her downy cheek, meanwhile taking in the odor of her body. She probably smelled like a child, but just that babyish quality made me feel she was a woman. I lifted her hair and kissed her earlobe. She just let me.

Afterwards I had qualms. I felt I'd behaved shamelessly. Besides, I just couldn't understand Etsuko. Did she really know nothing? In my confusion I made much too big a thing of having moistened her ear with my saliva. Somehow I was beginning to believe that there really were watermelon-sized cicadas at Karuizawa. Actually, though, the real fibber was Etsuko herself. Late that night I had a call from her.

"What's wrong? You're not feeling well?" I blurted into the receiver. She'd claimed she was sick, so perhaps what had happened that day had put her in a fever, and this was her retort.

"There are all these frogs jumping around, I can't sleep. There was something cold on my face, and I turned on the light. It was a tree frog. I can't imagine how they all got in, but they're all over my bed—tiny tree frogs, the size of the tip of your little finger."

I found that hard to swallow, and even if it *was* true, it was now nearly two in the morning. She must be doing this on purpose—in which case that *higurashi* had quite likely been another invention of hers. As though to confirm my suspicions, she then began trying the same sort of thing over and over again. For example, she'd insist on asking me, one by one, the names of trees, plants, animals, and such, then suddenly cackle with laughter and exclaim, "What a know-it-all you are! You pretend to know everything, don't you, with that solemn expression on your face!" At the same time she'd practically flaunt the yellow celluloid bracelet she wore.

It seemed to be typical of Etsuko to do the same thing over and over. She'd spend half a day on a single game of patience. Once, when the nutcracker was broken, I taught her to crack walnuts in the hinge of a door, the way I'd learned to do on a sports club outing in middle school. She couldn't get over it. At first she said she'd crack just three or four, to nibble on, but soon she was running breathlessly around the big dining room door, gleefully shouting, "See? See?" every time one cracked. "Mm, you're good, you're good!" I'd chime in. "All right, then, the *next* one!" she'd cry when she mashed meat and shell together, so carried away that her forehead, which she liked to think rarely perspired, was soon gleaming with sweat. Bang! Bang! went the heavy oaken door, on and on and on, while Specs, the astonished

dog, barked and barked. I ate too many walnuts that day, and my
head felt very strange.

I became more and more brazen. Soon it was my habit in the
morning, when my job was over, to head straight for Etsuko's place,
take a shower, and stretch out on the living room couch to sleep for
a while. I had the funny feeling, when I opened the front door and
went in, that the night watchman I had just been was now a burglar;
but once I awoke from my nap and Etsuko made me coffee, I might
easily complain about the coffee being a little weak. You could have
said the same about Etsuko herself. When she relaxed on the carpet
reading a book, feet tucked up beside her and one elbow propped
on a leather stool, I had the absentminded delusion that she'd grown
up in this house as the daughter of the family. Set into one wall
of the living room there was an alcove with seats in it, like a train
compartment, with at the end just the sort of fireplace Etsuko would
like. The hearth was heaped with black glass, to look like coal, with
colored electric lights inside it. When you turned it on, the black
glass glowed red from within, and green and yellow flames sprang
up as though it really was burning, but actually it gave off no heat at
all. It was just there for decoration.

"Let's take a train ride," we'd often say, and go to the alcove.

"We have to have our *bento*!" She'd bring some sweets.

"Goodness, look at Mount Fuji! It's so clear!" While we ate, she'd
point at the mountain scene hanging over the mantelpiece. But since
our facing chairs were about six feet apart, we'd end up sitting on the
floor. The "train" was the darkest place in the room anyway, being so
cut off, and around us the table, chairs, and so on would vanish into
blackness like that at the bottom of a mountain gorge, till only the
warm fireplace glow lit up that side of Etsuko's face. Sprawled there
on the carpet, I felt the deep pile clinging to me with a strange sort

of dampness, and meanwhile I recalled the sensation of touching my lips to Etsuko's now-ruddy earlobe. I got an itch to reach out and touch it, but for some reason I just couldn't, even though she was always right there. Well, I don't have to do exactly *that*, I began saying to myself. Could this be love? My first impression of Etsuko's face, and my present one, were completely different.

I soon became caught up in Etsuko's fantasy play. I enjoyed it. Going along with her stories made me feel as though I had taken possession of her. At her suggestion we played hide-and-seek. For all practical purposes, the house and everything in it belonged to us. There were hiding places everywhere—under the bed, behind the curtains, in the chest of drawers, in the dressing room with all its mirrors. I went upstairs and hid in a battlefield water bag that hung, unused, in the closet at the end of the hall. This was my bright idea. It wibble-wobbled around a lot while I was trying to climb into it, but it was quite comfortable once I got all the way in. I made a hole in the seam and peered through while Etsuko went up and down the hall any number of times without ever noticing me. In her wanderings she opened the bedroom door, then the dressing room door, then rushed with a shout into the bathroom, only to end up going back downstairs, calling my name and disappearing somewhere into the distance. At first I had to try very hard not to laugh, but eventually I got bored and I must have dozed off—after all, my job required me to stay up all night, and I was used to sleeping in the daytime. I don't know how long I slept. When I woke up, the house was strangely quiet. I started downstairs. Walking along the silent, high-ceilinged hallway, I noticed a dusty smell coming from around my shoulders. I opened the dining room door to find Etsuko sitting dejectedly at the table before an enormous jello pie.

"*There* you are!" she cried out in astonishment, instantly regaining all her animation. "This is a secret dessert recipe Mrs. Craigow taught me to make," she explained. "It's delicious, and you're not going to get *any*! You're horrid, so now I'm going to be horrid, too. And I only just made it this morning . . ."

I asked her not to talk that way, and begged her to let me have some. I was fully awake now, and while talking to her I'd become ravenously hungry.

"Nope. I'm going to eat it all myself."

"Please! Just a bite!" By the time I'd got that out she'd taken the pie, eight inches across, in both hands and lifted it to her mouth. Her tongue peeped out and licked the jello brimming from the crust.

I groaned with only half-feigned disappointment.

Through the cream on her lips she smiled mischievously. "How about you eating it from your side?" With the pie still in her mouth, she thrust it in front of me.

There was no time to think. Jello all over our faces, we kissed.

Colonel Craigow had been gone just four weeks.

Now I couldn't live without Etsuko. Everything unconnected with her seemed trivial. At the gun store I couldn't sit still. The owner would have been astonished to discover the worker his night watchman had become. Previously, as soon as the store was empty I would slump into the best chair in the place to read or doze, but now I couldn't stand being still for five minutes. I was always fidgeting about hither and yon, running my fingers along the gun racks, rattling away at the door and window locks, then finding myself in front of the ammunition room, reading the thermometer. Still, I doubt I would even have noticed a burglar. I was just waiting for Etsuko to call.

The telephone on the desk set my heart pounding whenever I sat still on the chair. Even in the toilet, I always had the feeling the phone might be ringing. At the same time, though, nothing put me more on edge than Etsuko's phone calls. Our endless chats, which lasted an hour or two or even more, frustrated me as though I'd been forced to stand outside a banquet, sniffing the aromas. All my words vanished into darkness, while hers reached me as no more than the insubstantial husk of speech. Meanwhile, we seemed to be engaged in a tug-of-war over something, though I couldn't tell what it was. She didn't get what I was saying, either. In the end she was reduced to a sort of animal cry, "Ooh-ow, ooh-ow, ooh-ow!"

At such times I'd want to bite right into the receiver, where the ghost of her voice lingered, as though it was a crust of bread.

We went around and around and around. The way we'd first kissed had clearly been a mistake. Perhaps we shouldn't have tried that until we were bored with more ordinary methods. There it was, though. Forever after, Etsuko's soft, slightly brownish hair and pale, almost liquid skin merged with that sugary, milky sweetness and clung to me day and night. I could only forget it was when I was actually touching her. No doubt her very childishness was the secret of her spell. What a problem that spell was, though! The dazzling fireworks display she'd set off might well have surprised even her. But did she really have to keep casting that same spell with every move?

"Just once! Just once!" she'd protest in my arms and draw away. Getting frantic did me no good. There was no strength in her resistance, but still there was nothing I could do. Eventually I'd go back to the store, still charged with pent-up tension. What could she possibly be thinking of me? Addicted as she was to this kind of nonsense, would she insist next on playing Big Bad Wolf? The next day I'd probably have to chase her all around the house and pretend to eat her from her toes all the way up to her head.

I was dazed. Sleep was practically impossible during the day, and I couldn't sleep at night, either, despite having lost any notion of responsibility for my job. When I was away from Etsuko, I'd be either jittering restlessly around or at the desk, my head on my arms, absorbed for some reason in visions of flying bullets.

Time passed terribly quickly. I didn't even notice. Perhaps because

I couldn't sleep, day and night became all mixed up, till I couldn't tell the difference between them, and they flitted through my head, overheated as it was with fretful anticipation, like one endless day. I was amazed. Etsuko ate nothing but cracker crumbs with milk over them. The wealth of food available to her had practically run out. Left on the shelves were pickled olives, anchovies, garlic, shredded coconut like dried-up, shaved *daikon* radish—stuff that we couldn't possibly eat. Specs ended up begging from the neighbors' kitchens. Our summer vacation was coming to an end.

There was this fellow called Hanayama. If you didn't know him, you'd have sworn when you saw him right after a bath that he'd fallen into a sewer or climbed through a manhole. He'd just been born with dirty blotches all over his skin. He didn't affect a grubby beard, though, or wear filthy shirts. On the contrary, he carried his own, personal mirror and, however penniless, never neglected to apply lotions and creams. The permed hair on his head was always as frizzy as the short hairs below. He wore pink-and-yellow striped drawers. "Made in USA!" he'd proclaim at the slightest excuse and want to drop his pants to show you. That was his idea of being a dandy. He kept shifting from one rented room to the next because everywhere he fell for some girl, invariably made a nuisance of himself, and had to move on. Every time he got himself a new girlfriend he'd show up at my place and test my patience by going on and on about her, half boasting and half complaining. It was strangely comical and at the same time sad, the way he waxed eloquent about matters of the heart while spewing saliva from the red mouth plunked into the middle of his pale, puffy face.

To me, however, this same Hanayama was now an expert on women. I told him all about what had been going on with Etsuko. Hallucinatory visions of her kept breaking into my interminable memories, rendering them more and more incoherent, till in the end I just cut myself off, gave Hanayama a pleading look, and asked, "What in the world am I going to do?"

Hanayama's answer was simple.

"What's the problem? It'll work out. Just one more try."

"It'll work out?"

I sounded as though I knew what he meant, but I had no idea. He gazed earnestly at me, then right to my face burst out laughing.

"You're hopeless!" He rocked with mirth, then suddenly stopped and added teasingly, "Look out, though. A woman's lies, however simpleminded, are still lies, and I wouldn't be surprised if you've just been had."

After Hanayama and I split up I went to town, to buy food to bring Etsuko. I'd borrowed all the money I could, and also sold my few books and dictionaries.

It felt like ages since I'd last walked around town. It was magnificently hot. The real summer was just beginning. The almost empty pantry shelves of the house in Harajuku spurred me on like the dwindling days on the calendar. We would have nothing left once the "summer vacation" was over. Clearly, everything would vanish without a trace, just as Cinderella's gown did at the stroke of midnight. Time was of the essence. At night, while busy waiting at the store, or when caught up in the games, by now hardly more than empty rituals, that Etsuko made us play, I realized that time, which had seemed to me less a burden than a veritable curse, was fast running out. Then suddenly I remembered that to buy something, you need only come up with the money. This simple thought stunned me like an oracle from on high. In my delight I experienced something of a hallucination: once the pantry was full again, the summer vacation would return.

Confusion suddenly assailed me in the food store. The big sausages and salted fish hanging from the ceiling, and the other foodstuffs massed along the walls, surrounded and overwhelmed me. This welter of grossly exposed eatables confounded me, as though I'd just been presented with a plate of sauce-drenched shoes. I'd never experienced such a feeling till I came to know Etsuko. Asking the price of this and that, and then paying, filled me with a sort of embarrassment. Even as I took the change from the moon-faced shop girl, I felt it just wasn't like me to be buying such stuff. I never realized, though, that the "me" in question was under Etsuko's influence. I just thought it was because I was doing all this for Etsuko. When I left the store with my armload of groceries, I felt as eager as a soldier cheered on by his general.

Colonel Craigow's house stood at the top of a slope, on a narrow alley leading off a broad, zelkova-lined avenue. The alley ended at the house. I climbed the slope with my load, sweating profusely under a golden sun, until to my huge relief the roof and windows popped into view. I found at the top, when I finally reached it, a big, khaki-roofed army truck. A jeep station wagon was pulled up on the slightly sloping ground in front of the entrance. It was Craigow's car. They were back. Never mind complaining that they were a week early. I suppose I was too tired to care, and I wasn't that devastated. I turned to leave. First, though, I had to get rid of all this stuff I was carrying, and that necessity encouraged me to risk taking a look.

Colonel Craigow stood in uniform on the porch, waving his pipe to direct the unloading of boxes great and small from the truck. Resolutely quelling my reluctance, I stepped through the gate. "US . . .": the white sign with the house-requisition order number on it suddenly loomed before me. "Guddo môningu!" I called loudly, still walking.

Instead of answering, the colonel glanced distastefully at me, his imposing, bushy-browed face set in a suspicious frown. That look did me in. I'd got the time wrong. It was two in the afternoon.

I remembered the electric clock with the thick hands I'd seen at the station and, unaccountably, felt desperate shame that gave way to a surge of fear. Turning on my heel, I ran so fast I practically tumbled down the hill.

The thermometer read thirty-four degrees centigrade. It was so hot, the DANGER painted in red outside the ammunition room looked ready to melt and run.

After my flight down that Harajuku slope, indescribable shame and self-loathing drove Etsuko from my mind for the rest of the day. Once I'd calmed down a bit, I realized that no degree of ingenuity could restore the life I'd led till just the day before yesterday; then anguish over Etsuko became an unbearable torment. My hopes in that direction, however intense, were doomed to failure. That little sign with the requisition number on it made it all too plain that she'd fallen into the hands of the enemy.

All I did was pace around the store. I had nothing, nothing whatsoever, left to wait for. The pyramid-shaped pile of cartridges still empty of powder, the little fireworks for school festivals, the wooden duck decoys—my gaze slid absently over them all.

About eleven o'clock a bell rang loudly. With a wry smile I rushed to the phone. The old habit was still alive; my heart was pounding. The next instant, though, everything changed. It wasn't the phone at all. Beyond the glass entrance door, visible past the raised blind, someone was standing out there under the street lamp. It was Etsuko. I tried to unlock the door, but the key just wouldn't go into the hole. She smiled through the glass when she recognized me. The orange light of the street lamp turned her face a scary gray. I could hardly believe it even after I got the door open, and she was in beside me. Her voice came through the striped shadows cast by the guns in their racks.

"It feels as though I haven't seen you for years."

She seemed to be speaking from a completely different world.

After suddenly returning the day before, Colonel Craigow and his wife had apparently left again today. Exhausted by their journey, they'd gone to Nikko for rest and relaxation.

"You're surprised?" Etsuko asked, watching my expression. "They say they'll be home the day after tomorrow. We have two more days of vacation."

I couldn't answer. She'd asked me whether I was surprised, but my astonishment was beyond words. Just when I thought I'd been shut out from that life, here it was back again. I felt as though I'd found a glass slipper. These two miraculous days were like a glass slipper dropped by the previous vacation. They gave me back everything I'd lost.

"They left early this morning. I phoned you right away, but I couldn't get you."

I wasn't available on the phone during the day. I couldn't be in the store. Etsuko should have known that.

"Oh, I see!" she exclaimed artlessly when I told her, rolling her eyes. At last the Etsuko I knew came back to me.

"I had a terrible time finding this place, you know."

I hadn't told her where the store was. She'd discovered the address on the old catalog used to wrap up the shotgun shells I'd delivered on my first visit to Harajuku.

"You'd have found it right away if you'd asked around the station."

"Mm, but for some reason I didn't want to."

She leaned her shoulders against my chest, and I put my arms around her. Her chest was heaving. Then she asked me to remove the big pipe I kept in my left breast pocket. Somewhat annoyed, I took it right out and tossed it on the floor. It clattered dryly on the fake stone. I took her the back of the store, where there was a leather couch. With Etsuko clinging to me and hampering my movements, I nearly fell time after time as I threaded my way past the showcases. If I had, we'd never have been able to get up again.

I was sure of it now. After this, life without Etsuko would be impossible. The time had come for us two to merge completely. All hesitation gone, I buried my face in her soft hair, so oblivious to the flames of consuming passion that I was thunderstruck when she pushed away the hand groping at her skirt. It had to be a mistake.

"We mustn't, we mustn't!" She deflected my hand again.

My first feeling was shame. For a second I blushed and grinned, but anger instantly followed. "You've got to be kidding!" I shouted, thrusting her hand back. "What did you come here for, then?" I was so furious I could have strangled her. That didn't last long either, though. Despite my rage, all the strength went out of me. I didn't resist when she brushed my hand away yet again. Still worse, she lay there wide-eyed like a shattered, discarded doll. Her thin legs dangled, as though broken, from beneath her skirt. I began to panic at the sight, like a fleet suddenly obliged to change formation in the midst of battle. My doubts went back to the start of our "summer vacation," when she'd claimed the *higurashi* cicada was a bird. And now, I realized, my error lay fully exposed: Etsuko was a complete and utter virgin. In my clasping arms, Etsuko's body became strangely heavy, as heavy as stone, and suddenly the couch felt terribly small. I just gazed up at the dark hole of the ceiling, meanwhile pressing a burning cheek against the couch back. The leather's grainy texture felt good.

Eventually Etsuko got up again. She tidied her hair before the glass of a showcase.

"There's a big mirror over there, if you want one!" I called from where I lay on the couch, startling myself as I did so. Wasn't I aiding and abetting her preparations to leave? Everything was slipping away from me, yet again.

I stood up, showed her to the mirror, and turned on the light. Being kind enough to give in to her had only meant losing her. In the glare her skinny back, with the wrinkles in her dress between the prominent shoulder blades, conveyed an unbearable sadness.

I started to say something but gave up. I wanted to put in a word, but I had none. Whatever I said would only ring hollow. If I let her go, she might well disappear beyond my reach, but speaking probably wouldn't help. With my own hands I would only be cutting the bond between us.

She turned away from the mirror. "Will you walk me back to the station?" she said with an innocent smile.

That was too much. "No! No way! Absolutely not!"

Everything goes on as usual at the gun shop. That's what's really surprised me. About all I do now is doze. I no longer feel like doing anything at all.

I wake from a nap, and there's the telephone on the desk. Up I jump and clap the receiver to my ear.

Silence.

I can't hear a thing. I hold onto the receiver, though. I press it to my ear and wait. Soon a faint, high-pitched murmur, like telephone wires brushing each other in the wind, teases the depths of my ear. It isn't words, of course. Still, it gradually grows louder, and it *does* sound like a voice. What is it whispering to me?

I just stay like that, receiver in hand. It's such fun, being fooled.

Homework

I was in fifth grade when I moved from an elementary school in Hirosaki to Aoyama South school in Tokyo. Aoyama South was famous because a lot of students went on from there to Tokyo Metropolitan Middle School. To get me in, my mother made a big fuss about moving to Tokyo before my father was transferred to a new office. She firmly believed that to get into Tokyo Imperial University I'd have to get into Tokyo Metropolitan Middle School, and that the only way to do that was for me to go to Aoyama South. Once I was in, though, she assumed, like any proper bureaucrat's wife, that the target middle school would be no problem at all.

At Hirosaki, the teacher and I were the only ones who could read the textbook in standard Japanese pronunciation, and that was all it took for me to rate at the top of the class. Sometimes the teacher would try to spur on the best among the students who'd already been there when I came. "Don't let Yashioka get ahead of you!" he'd say; but on that terrain, try as they might, they could never keep up with me. So reading the textbook remained my specialty even after we moved to Tokyo. Whenever I did so, the class would fall dead silent.

I had no idea it was because my accent was actually a muddle of Shikoku and Tohoku dialects and the speech favored in the colonies. Still, I did all right at reading. I hadn't a clue about math or science, though. Sure enough, toward the end of the first semester of fifth year, my class at South Aoyama was already getting into the sixth-year curriculum. The teacher reprimanded me in due form for being so hopeless, but none of it got through. All he did was make me stand endlessly in front of my desk. Hirosaki wasn't like this. The school building there was a former barracks, and the classroom was separated from the corridor by a row of rifle racks. A student who earned the teacher's wrath was put in a real brig. We thought nothing of it. Some kids would crow "cock-a-doodle-doo" just to annoy him when he went to let them out.

The first semester was over before I knew it. Surprisingly, every grade on my school report was an A. This, as I found out only quite a bit later, was for the benefit of the middle school.

The summer vacation in Tokyo was interminable. In Hirosaki it lasted from August first to August thirty-first, but in Tokyo it began instead on July twentieth. One day I took a taxi to Kamakura, but otherwise I was always at home alone, and I really got sick of it. I had ten notebooks full of homework assignments to do for every subject, but I didn't even open them. I didn't even know what homework was. At school, they set up a Health and Exercise Week for the kids who weren't going to the seaside or to the country. They'd stand them there, naked, on the asphalt playground and hose them with water. I went there just three days. I liked "T-straps," as the shoes some girls wore were called—the ones with a strap buttoned at the ankle. They could make a girl look pretty. There were no mixed classes, but this was vacation time, and we played games together. In the afternoon there were magic shows, comic skits, storytelling, or talking movies. I sat next to a girl wearing T-straps and watched her. When the lights went out, waves of brightness washed over the screen—a grubby, yellowish curtain—and on came the grainy shapes of warships. Rippling across the screen, they thrust forth their great guns, from the tips of which burst puffs of white smoke. I put up a show of glancing back at the projector and secretly stole a look at the girl next to me. Her face loomed, pale in the flickering dazzle of the carbon arc lamp, and she smelled vaguely of milk. The film clattered along for a while, then suddenly the nearby loudspeaker went Boom! as the guns fired, and abruptly the lights came on. The girl smiled at me in surprise. Next, we began playing make-believe. The same girl assigned me my role. "This guy's the modern boy from the country," she declared. That stuck with me. When we ran around the playground, our sweaty bodies got all grimy, and I felt as though the grime clinging to *me* gave me a special country stink. I tried and tried to hose it off, but I always got dirty again right away.

My cousin Sadaka celebrated her wedding during that same summer vacation. The event took place at Gakushikai Hall in Kanda. Earlier, I'd gone out for a western-style dinner with my parents, and afterwards my mother had told me my table manners were so bad, she'd felt embarrassed in front of the waiter; so the wedding banquet made me terribly nervous. Things didn't go as I expected, though. For the first time in my life I saw a Shinto priest. Dressed in pale blue robes, a black lacquered *eboshi* hat, and wooden clogs, and issuing orders to a woman in a white top and red *hakama* trousers who was apparently an underling, he looked to me like a magician. When he swished the white purification streamers over my head, I was sure I caught a whiff of the gods. Then he turned to the altar and began groaning out meaningless sounds. His voice was so strange that I thought it came from outdoors.

"It's weird, Mom," I whispered. "There's a cow mooing."

My mother paled and shook her head emphatically, but it was too late. A wave of laughter swept the room, and as the chief offender

I was sent out. Desperately embarrassed, I raced up to the roof, from where dizzying vistas stretched before me, crawling with ant-like cars and trolleys. The thought that I'd get none of the banquet I'd been so worried about made it seem unbearably delicious. A few days later Sadaka's uncle, who'd been there at the wedding, shot himself to death with a pistol.

By and large the family name Imobe, which sounded as though it meant "Spudman," made my cousins seem pretty strange. The Imobes had once been a wealthy rural family, but now there were just three of them living in a third-floor apartment in Aoyama: my aunt, Sadaka, and Jû-chan, a freshman at Tokyo Imperial University. Sadaka and Jû's father had lost a lot of money in the stock market before I started school, and he had died by his own hand. My aunt was proud of the way they'd used to live, and what impressed me even more than her talk of peacocks in the garden was her insisting that in the way of underwear she never let my cousin Jû wear anything but a flannel wrap. Apparently that was why Jû-chan remained afraid of wearing underwear even after he started school, so that he never took part in school athletic meets. That's the sort of thing that, for me, made him such an odd mixture of babyish and grown-up. He loved sumo wrestling, and he had a wooden tangerine box full of wrestler dolls cut out of graph paper. He'd whack his desk loudly while he made them fight each other. I'd have died of embarrassment if my name had been Imobe Shigematsu, but he claimed that the *I Ching* sanctioned it as perfect, and he'd written it out with a brush and pasted it up everywhere, even on his desk and his bookcase, like a protective talisman. At times like that he could be as fussy as an old man. As a cousin I didn't especially like him, but we got on well in some ways, and at times I felt I even resembled him. This stuff makes you smarter, he'd say, and stealthily open his drawer to show me, and me alone, a bottle of blue liquid and some pills in a tin.

It was late one afternoon. The sun was going down, and summer vacation was about half over. We'd nearly finished dinner when a voice called from the entrance. My mother and I went to see who it was and found Jû-chan—as the family called Shigematsu—standing there all by himself. His face was in shadow, and we couldn't see his eyes or mouth.

"Auntie," he said, "read this." He held out a telegram that rattled in his shaking hand. I had no idea what had him in such a fright. An uncle of theirs had lost everything on the stock market, and as a result had shot both his children with a pistol before committing suicide. It was the same pistol Jû-chan's own father had killed himself with. After hearing all this, I still couldn't understand why he was trembling so. Forever after, Jû-chan's face, with his bulging forehead that looked as though you were seeing it through gray water and his dark eyes glimpsed through thick, near-sighted lenses, always made me vaguely uneasy.

Every day dragged by. Talking to Jû-chan was a bore, and playing ball with the neighborhood kids—the sons of a temple carpenter and a Tenrikyô priest—was no fun either. They went not to Aoyama South, but to Yama Elementary School, a good distance away. Our playground was a big vacant lot that we called "Mr. Shimazu's." I used to climb up on the fence and eat furry grey loquats from the neighbor's tree. I got tired of Mr. Shimazu's too, though, when the loquats gave out. Every afternoon the public bath was full of kids nobody took even to the Tama River, let alone to the beach. Some brought rubber water wings or a brightly painted, handmade wooden submarine. To me, it all looked stupid. Just once I impressed them all by staying underwater for a count of one hundred, but otherwise, "dumb" was their word for everything I did. This didn't especially annoy me. For all I knew, they were right.

I was bored. It didn't bother me to be rejected by the bunch who gathered at the bath, but there was something eating away at me. At first I didn't mean to cheat, but one day the cashier lady gave me the wrong change. Everything would have been fine if she'd given me one *sen* back on the five *sen* coin I gave her on the way in, but she actually gave me six *sen*. Mad with joy, I rushed out of the bath house and straight to a cheap candy shop, where after a moment's hesitation I blew my windfall on Shintaka bubble gum. I didn't like chewing gum, and I was so frightened when I peeled off the waxed paper and popped it into my mouth that I might have been swallowing fire. The Shintaka lumps were unusually large, and you couldn't move your tongue at all once you took in a whole one. It wasn't far to where I lived. After spitting the thing out at our gate, I realized that I should have kept one *sen* to give my mother, as she expected, so I decided to claim I'd forgotten to take the change. She just believed me. The next day, though, I could think of nothing but how much fun it was to cheat. At first the cashier woman returned a single *sen*, but when I stood there without a word, she picked up a five-*sen* coin and gave it to me, still looking toward the baths. This time I made sure I kept my spending to exactly five *sen*. I did it again the next day, then the day after that and the day after that. It kept on going. Every day I bought chewing gum. Five *sen* worth of gum was too much to finish on the way home, and to get through it I'd have to keep chewing even in bed. In the end the gum was no fun to chew, and it drove me crazy, the way the lump always stayed exactly the same size.

It was as though I spent the whole day swathed in bath steam, amid the clink and clank of buckets. The thought of the cashier lady put me in a bad mood, whatever I was doing, and I'd go up to the second floor to lie down. Eventually the sun would come pouring in onto the tatami, till the soles of my feet itched. The time had come at last. Soap and towel in hand, I'd feel my chest fill with inexpressible hope, as though I'd swallowed a great weight of water. Well, maybe today's the day! I'd say to myself. But all that ever happened was that, as always, she gave me back five *sen* too much. In bed at night I'd wake up from dreams of demons dragging me off by the hair. I'd turn on the light, to find my head glued to the covers by chewing gum.

At the public bath I'd meet my classmate Ôkuma. His voice sounded like a *Naniwa-bushi* ballad singer's, and he did everything else, too, just like a grownup. Even at the bath he'd wring out his towel expertly before using it to wash his back, and he'd rap smartly on his water bucket before emptying it over himself. He was also a pretty good student at school, and he never once annoyed a teacher. His hairline receded a little, so that when he sat there nodding at what the teacher was saying, there could have been an old man in the classroom.

Ôkuma folded his polka dot–patterned towel, draped it over his head, closed his eyes, and stretched out in the bath to soak. I flopped into the water beside him, and he opened his eyes a little and asked, "Well, have you done your homework? Only eight more days of vacation."

I was amazed. With this word or two, Ôkuma had suddenly admitted me to the company of the Tokyo students. At last I felt the weight of responsibility for my homework. "Not yet," I answered in a small voice. I didn't have it in me to say more. I'm sure there was plenty I'd have liked to ask him, but that mountainous pile of homework, the one I'd just left heaped up in my room, burst into my mind, and I couldn't think of a thing. Back home again, I stealthily opened my assignment book, making sure no one was looking. My gaze slid over all those characters, and I had no idea what they meant. Over and over I heard Ôkuma's voice saying, "Have you done your homework? Only eight more days of vacation," and all I knew was that I was in big trouble. There was sukiyaki for dinner, but the meat wouldn't go down. I remembered cousin Jû-chan assuring me that eating raw scallions made you smarter, so I picked out for myself only the least cooked bits of scallion. I was too restless to stay at the table once the meal was over, but I couldn't bear the idea of going upstairs and facing that assignment book. For one thing, my mother would undoubtedly be surprised to see me at my desk after dinner, with the light on. Her ignorance of the ways of Tokyo elementary school students surpassed even my own. Besides, she was much keener on my school than I was, so she'd be even more worried than me if she saw that totally blank assignment book and realized it was for my summer vacation homework. To start studying now was hopeless.

"I'll just have to stay up all night," I said to myself. "Stay up all night" was a favorite expression of Jû-chan's, and it always impressed me. I'd have to hide it, of course, so I lay in bed and waited till my parents were asleep. Once everything was quiet, I'd start by sneaking out onto the laundry-drying platform and take a few deep breaths. And then, and then . . . I imagined each step as I lay there, eyes wide open in the dark, but I kept hearing talking. Silence never fell. Sometimes I closed my eyes a little. I didn't fall asleep, though. It never got quiet enough for me to sneak out safely. And then, to my amazement, there was the sun, beating down on that same drying platform. Every morning I'd go out on the platform, look up at the sky, and sigh with regret over the failure of my plan.

Each day was a little shorter than the last. Even I could tell that evening was coming earlier and earlier. Fearful of looking like a lazybones for lolling around upstairs, I'd pretend to play busily outside while I waited for night. It's impossible to describe my feelings when it got dark. Each day's departure made my homework burden that much heavier, and the approach of that hated time when I would have to study made my heart as black as the night itself. After dinner I'd go straight to bed. The very idea of the perils that awaited me when I got up in the middle of the night made me too nervous to stay up at all. To keep my eyes open in bed I'd chew away desperately at my gum, and the mint flavor in my mouth filled me with nostalgia for those still so recent days when I could indulge in forgetting about the whole thing.

Day followed day in the blink of an eye, and in no time there was just one day left till the beginning of school. That afternoon I had a fight with the neighboring carpenter's kid. I got beaten and bloodied. I'd never had a real fight like that before. He'd already moved on to a higher grade, but when we were playing as usual at Mr. Shimazu's he'd come over from time to time and drop some remark on me, like, "My little sister's called Kumeko, coz she was such a big baby," then drift off again without another word, looking bored. I climbed Mr. Shimazu's persimmon tree by myself and thought of the fable about the crab who had planted a persimmon tree and the lazy monkey who wanted to eat all the ripe fruit. I didn't play baseball. When everyone was playing together and it was my turn to bat, they'd all pretend to forget, then skip me. That was fine by me. What did bother me was that my mother might come by. There's nothing worse than having someone you know see you standing there alone, ignored by everyone else. To keep that from happening, I straddled a branch of the tree and made a great show of having a good time tearing off the green persimmons and tossing them away. Before I knew it, there was the carpenter's kid down there in his soiled clothes, hands stuck in his belt, looking up at me. But why? In a sudden flash of annoyance, I crunched down on a mouthful of persimmon and spat it out. The kid said something or other. "So you're scarfing up persimmons, are you?" Those were probably more or less his words, but all I actually heard was a string of meaningless syllables, and his disapproving look irked me. I scuttled down from the tree at breakneck speed, barefoot, and lit into him. Being much stronger, he ended up straddling me in a depression of the uneven ground next to the crumbling tile wall. I thrashed my legs about, struggling with might and main to throw him off, but I succeeded only in digging my shoulders deeper into the soft soil. I tried spitting at him, but he just stuffed a lump of red dirt into my mouth. I had dirt in my nose, dirt in my ears, dirt in my eyes and all over my face. When at last I thought I *had* thrown him off, he'd simply stood up and left, with a contemptuous glance at the other excited kids. I grabbed some rocks and threw a few after him, but they missed.

One shirt sleeve was torn off at the shoulder, and I was covered with mud and blood. What bothered me more than the pain was what I'd say to my mother. My mother, however, was less angry than simply aghast. I got some money and went straight the public bath. But misfortune never strikes only once. It was a ten-*sen* coin I'd received this time, whereas all the other times I'd been to the bath, I'd got just five *sen*. I never even noticed the difference till I gave the cashier the coin. On my way out, the woman gave me back only one *sen* in change. I stood there forever, but in vain. She kept staring at me and pushing the copper one *sen* coin toward me across the zelkova-wood counter. No, it was no good. The little swindle I'd managed with some surprise to keep going so long was well and truly over. I understood how extraordinarily lucky I'd been. Suspecting that this incident now foreshadowed future disasters, I walked straight past the familiar candy store.

At home again, I felt compelled to announce, "We all swim around in there so much, they decided to charge us ten *sen* today." This worked amazingly well. My mother just laughed. She even seemed to have forgotten all about the fight. In fact, she so merrily told our neighbor the story that I got a little nervous about it.

The last day of the summer vacation happened to be festival day at Zenkôji Temple, out on the streetcar avenue. After sunset the place was packed with people. My father was away (they were always sending him off somewhere), and I went there with my mother to see what was going on. A kid named Saigô hailed me as we were passing Mr. Shimazu's lot. At dodgeball Saigô, short but sturdy, could smoke one straight at you, harder than any of the others. It was odd to hear him calling my name. This chance meeting as the long vacation drew to a close suggested a mutual warmth, as though we'd found each other on an expedition into the mountains. Saigô had come with his older sister. We parted as boys do, with just a few, simple words, and as he was leaving, I heard his sister ask him who I was. Saigô answered, and despite the distance I distinctly caught her reply. "What a nice friend for you!" she said.

That really pleased me. I felt as though by the flickering lights of all those shops and stalls I had, for the first time since moving to Tokyo, found a friend. I even thought of presenting Saigô with half the treasured Sarutobi Sasuke pictures I'd collected in Hirosaki. The Zenkôji Temple main hall stood out like fireworks, it was so crammed with burning incense sticks and candles. Walking along like that, hand in hand with my mother, I chattered away like a drunk. Talk about indiscretion! After being so careful all that time, I'd started carrying on like mad about my friends and even about school, embroidering on the subject as I talked. The temple grounds were a mass of stalls. The protective talisman bags with little bells on them, the mentholated pipes, the newly invented *daikon* graters left me cold, but I liked the automatic pencils made of tin. Their mechanism for extending the red and the blue wasn't like the ones sold in stationery stores, and the man in the dark glasses took them reverently from their box, one by one, to demonstrate how easily they wrote, no matter how you held them, by holding them straight or slantwise to draw endless circles, triangles, and wavy lines. I could have stood there forever, but my mother tugged me away. I hated to go.

"One of those'd be so great for coloring in maps!"

It worked. Still, my mother hadn't quite put her hand to the purse she kept in the fold of her kimono. I jiggled her hand.

"Drawing maps is part of my homework!"

She looked at me. Nearly there! Mindlessly excited, I went on, "I have tons to do! I have piles of vacation homework!"

A stern glitter entered my mother's eyes as she paid. Then she handed me the cool pencil, and I understood that I'd at last fallen into the trap I'd taken such pains to dig for myself. I wanted to get back home just as fast as possible. That was all, though.

My mother had never caught on. With all my fidgeting about, she'd make the mistake of thinking I was just having a good time.

The sight of my blank assignment book, dated July twenty-first, gave her a good start, but greater misery even than mine suddenly overcame her when every page of the nine notebooks that followed turned out to be as white as snow. She began to cry, and I didn't know what to do.

"Why don't you just die?" she said. "That's what *I'm* going to do."

To me, that sounded like a good idea. She told me to go and get the gas hose, but when I started toward the kitchen for it, she suddenly dragged me to my desk, sat me down, and clutched a notebook herself, pencil in hand. This was it. My mother and I began applying ourselves frantically to filling my assignment book from cover to cover. We couldn't afford a minute's break. By the time my arm felt like a dead weight and the pencil was nearly slipping from my fingers, I'd finally understood how to do homework. Now I could write without getting lost. I decided to write only the answers to the math questions. Writing the figures alone, I could answer as many as seven questions a minute, even when the problem required amazing multiplications up to twenty-three digits long. When it came to practical problems like deriving the values of two unknown quantities, such as the numbers of cranes and tortoises, from their unit total and the total of one of their attributes, I didn't even have to read the question. I could just write down, "Ten cranes, three tortoises." That did just as well as thinking about it and getting the answer wrong anyway. I began zipping through them impressively fast, while my mother struggled to keep up.

"Name nine major marine products of Hokkaido, giving for each the place where it is harvested and the quantity taken annually." *That* one really annoyed her, but she began writing anyway, in large letters, "Kelp, tuna, bonito . . ."

Dawn came before I even knew it. Staying up all night, which had seemed so mighty a feat, turned out to be nothing at all. Tomorrow had just disappeared and was now today. I felt cheated. The sun shining through the morning mists would be nice and warm. The homework was done at seven, which was perfect. Any earlier, and I might have started worrying about my wacky answers.

On the first day of September there were no classes. In the classroom, the class president just collected the homework. This was a kid who had once sent me out to buy bread for him during the lunch break. No doubt he wanted me to know how demanding a job it was, being class president. I wasn't meaning to get back at him or anything, but what I bought him was "octopus bread"—bread shaped like a dancing octopus. His mother was upset when she came to bring him his sandwich and found him with octopus bread. That made him nervous, and he threatened me with a belligerent glare. For some reason, when he came around to collect the assignment books he put mine on the very bottom. Perhaps it was just chance, but anyway, I was more relieved than anything else to see my faked homework go that far down.

When all the homework was in, the teacher, Mr. Kanehara, said, "Your vacation is over now, and it's going to be nothing but work, work, work for you till you get through the college entrance exams the year after next. Your future depends on them, so no more vacations."

"Your future depends on them": that was the refrain at Aoyama South. It came up at every ceremony, at every morning assembly, on every other formal occasion, and with every reprimand you ever got. We all concluded our compositions, no matter what the subject, with "The exams on which our future depends . . ." Mr. Kanehara's face was not like most people's—his jaw jutted out squarely below his ears. His boxlike chin moved when he talked, and his big front teeth stuck out, till you thought you'd be bitten if you got too close. I was starting to become genuinely afraid of him. I hadn't felt that way before the vacation. He cruised around among our desks, slapping his indoor slippers hard against the floor, talking as he went.

"Has anyone *not* brought his homework today?" The culprits were ordered to stand up. With a mixture of worry and relief I watched a number of students rise, rattling the metal fittings on their desks as they did so, and among them I was surprised to see Ôkuma. Mr. Kanehara gave them a perfunctory glance.

"Very well," he said. That was all. Then seat reassignment began. I got one in the fifth row from the front, right in the middle of the classroom. The ten students who'd stood up all got end seats, as far as possible from the windows. Then school was over. I had no idea what it was all about. Usually the teacher kept you standing the whole hour when you'd forgotten just a day's worth of homework, but even that didn't happen. And the strangest of all was this business of Ôkuma. I thought about him all the way home. The teacher knew he was a good student—was that why he'd let him off? It was so peculiar, though, that none of the others had been scolded either. Even Piggy Suzuki got off without a tongue-lashing—it was hardly possible! So presumably the homework hadn't been that important. Ôkuma must have just wanted to give me, the country bumpkin, a scare. All he'd asked was, "Have you done your homework?" I could have answered, "Nope!" and that would have been that. At Hirosaki, no one had even heard of homework. The teachers themselves never used the word. So it was true, then: even at a Tokyo school they didn't make a big deal of it either. If it was a crime not to do your homework, then that school in Hirosaki was a den of thieves, and the classrooms there didn't need a single chair, since chairs were only for students who disliked standing so much that they always turned in their homework. Those were the guys who were weak in the legs and couldn't take it. And I was the only one who hadn't known. Ôkuma and the others who hadn't brought in their homework that day—they were the ones who were headed for high school. They could goof off all they liked, and no one would say a word. On the other hand, they could study all they liked and still never get all A's. Those places on the class ranking list went to others.

Had the classroom changed, or was it me? Every day I went to school, to stand, but meanwhile I had the feeling there was something different about the place. At the start of each class the teacher would have us put our open notebooks on our desks, then come around to see whether or not we'd done our homework for the day. He made those who hadn't stand. Then he'd head straight into tackling the homework questions, and those who'd gotten them wrong had to stand for a while. Kawamoto, the deputy class president, got a math problem wrong once and had to stand up. Tall as he was, he leaned his hands on his desk and looked about to cry. I couldn't figure it out. What was his problem? He'd be sitting down again in no time, so he had it a lot easier than me, didn't he, when I had to stand the whole hour? I reflected that how things look to you depends on how you take them, and you could be perfectly happy even while having a tough time. Lately, however, I'd really begun to hate just standing there feeling stupid. This had nothing to do with my now fearing that mouth of Mr. Kanehara's, which opened like a box. It was a strange, oppressive feeling, a feeling like boredom, although it didn't make me yawn. Before, I'd thought of all sorts of things while I stood there: skiing down a slope into an apple orchard with branches sticking up like thorns through the snow, the bride alighting from her sleigh, the hair on her legs, Jû-chan's flannel wrap, jumping rope, shoes, kicking rocks . . . All this bubbled up in my head like the foam spit up by a crab. Now, though, nothing came at all. I didn't even wish that the time would go faster, or that I could eat my lunch. I didn't want to play games. No, now it was the teacher's voice that was getting to me. Everything he said seemed to come down to, "You're a nuisance, you're a nuisance," and I felt alone and useless. If I didn't at least keep my own head completely empty, I'd have nowhere to go at all.

That morning I set off once again for school, to stand. I'd gone down the street in front of our house and was about to turn the corner when I ran into a boy about two years younger than me, coming out of his gate with his mother. He was wearing a hat with a neck protector on it, and she was adjusting his rucksack. Then off he raced, as lively as could be. The sight was so cheery and bracing that I even felt like doing the same myself. After running a few steps, though, I quit. A *good* boy took care of his homework. All I wanted was somewhere to hide. I could hardly go back home now. Arriving late for class was nothing, but I was sure my mother would cry again, like last time, if she saw me start studying in the morning. She seemed perfectly calm, as though she'd forgotten all about my homework once the summer vacation was over. The kids strolling or rushing to school thinned out, and finally there I was at the fateful corner—a right turn would put me smack in front of the school. I hurried straight ahead. It's *bad* boys who don't do their homework, I kept telling myself. Not doing your homework's the *worst*.

Down that path lurked dangers. I pretended to have forgotten something and ran on and on, away from my house, away from my school. Long walls stretched endlessly along both sides of the road, with never a sign of any dark, narrow, comforting side street. Then, suddenly, there just off the road was a cemetery amid dense trees. I was so relieved, I even forgot this was where General Nogi's tomb was. This cemetery in the middle of Aoyama, surrounded by houses that pressed in on it from all sides, was actually a spacious wood.

I headed for the thickest growth I could find, afraid someone might be after me. I wasn't that scared of ghosts. Still, I didn't think any other kid could do it. Right inside the graveyard there was a menthol-like chill, and the air smelled of green tangerines. There were bugs everywhere. The damp earth was crawling with earwigs and woodlice. Huge spiders, bursting with poison, were sailing through the stagnant air on invisible threads. I looked for a spot to do my homework, found a recumbent Christian gravestone on which I spread out my assignment book, sat myself down on my rucksack, and was about to begin when I discovered dozens of mosquitoes sucking away at my shorts-clad legs. Covered in blood from their stings, I grabbed my books and ran for my life. And then I remembered an awful truth. I could perfectly well just have spent today standing and done my homework for tomorrow.

In the end, I never got to school that day. Time passed far more quickly for me, alone in the graveyard, than it ever did in the classroom among all the other kids. At the sound of the noon siren I ate my lunch, then my worries began to drop away, and I strolled about in sunny places. Going home was a problem, though. I started walking just a little before the time school let out, assembling meanwhile in my head all the plausible stories I could think of. A policeman spotted me when I came to the familiar intersection. I'd never noticed the police box there before. If he questioned me, I'd tell him I was going home because I was ill; so I walked slowly along, trying hard not to be frightened and doing my best to look as weak as possible. When I finally got home, I threw open the front door and announced my return in a purposely cheery voice, as a prelude to rushing up to my room. Most unfortunately my mother, who knew nothing, was lying drowsily in the dim interior of the house. Smiling as though completely taken in by my bouncy act, she said, "Before you take your shoes off, won't you go and order us some shaved ice with sweet bean topping?" I most certainly didn't want any just then, but how could I possibly say so? At this very moment, hundreds of Aoyama South students were crowding through the streets. All I could do was stand there, grinning beatifically.

The next day, I went to school as usual. I assumed I'd get by without having to stand. In the process of checking homework as always, Mr. Kanehara headed toward my desk. You could always tell he was coming, even from behind, by his smell. A mingled soap and pickled radish odor preceded him on the chilly air, and his shoes squeaked. He reached out and leafed through my brown assignment book. The white pages were all blank. He plopped the book back down on my desk. I made no move to stand. He looked at me. I'd been meaning to say, "I was sick yesterday, there was no way I could know we had homework for today," but nothing happened when I tried to move my lips. It was like in dream, when you can't make a sound. Mr. Kanehara stared at me with his doglike eyes, then turned his back on me. Much against my own wishes, I stood up. Back at the podium, he began going through the math problems as usual, opening and closing those front teeth of his. Absolutely nothing had changed.

Every morning on the way to school I'd wonder what to do. I'd walk along deep in thought. I'd kick a pebble. If it hit the electric pole, I'd go to school. It hit the pole. Strange to tell, however, every time that happened my grandfather would turn up—the one who was such a stickler for thrift and good manners that the rest of the family was afraid of him. He should have been in the country, but no: with his speckled face and a white scarf around his neck he'd suddenly appear through a crack in a garden wall or from under a pine tree and mumble as though sucking on candy, "Go to the graveyard!" That was all. Then he'd disappear. So I had to give up the idea of going to school. My grandfather had once astonished the whole family by presenting me with five yen.

For some reason a lot started going on in the cemetery. My first day there was the only time I ever tried to use a gravestone as a desk to do my homework. After that I'd find some deserted thicket and play hide-and-seek with myself. The mosquitoes were so bad that now and again I'd go out onto the broad, paved road that ran through the middle. The cemetery was all dips and rises, so the road went up and down, too. At first I got a terrible scare whenever anyone came by. When from the bottom of a hollow I saw someone coming down the slope, wearing a red armband, I rushed to hide behind the hedge around a tombstone, but it was only an old groundskeeper with a broom. I couldn't afford to be careless, though, even with him. Some boy in his own family might be going to Aoyama South, and if that boy was a class president or something, this old man for all I knew might be on good terms with the teacher and report me. But I overdid my caution. When the groundskeeper suddenly appeared, not coming down the slope but from right behind a gigantic stone funerary monument, I didn't have time to get out of sight. Yelling and brandishing his broom, he came right after me into the shrubbery, presumably convinced I was some sort of rascal stealing money from the offertory boxes. I got away that time, but it would actually have been safer if I'd gone out onto the road. There were never many people on the road in the first place.

The next morning, though, there were big footprints everywhere around my favorite tomb. The fence around it was so high you couldn't see in, there weren't that many bugs, and there was nice grass to lie on. Unfortunately, it was no place for me now. I could only go on to my second favorite tomb, where I found footprints just like the first. In fact, there were even more of them. At the third tomb there was a confusion of wooden *geta* sandal and shoe prints, together with sweets wrapped in fresh paper and incense that was still burning. This discovery astonished me more than it alarmed me or put me off. Wandering around looking for somewhere to hide, I ran most unusually into people dressed in their best. On the big road there were a lot of black cars, and as noon approached, far from being able to rest, I found I had practically no refuge left. On narrow paths normally frequented only by mosquitoes, I ended up being caught between groups of four or five people, one behind me and one ahead. It was hopeless. I hid my rucksack in a thicket of dwarf bamboo and pretended to be a bored child stuck with having to go along on a visit to the family graves.

Hanging around listening to a young wife, as I supposed she was, and an older woman chatting together, I finally gathered what day this was. The young woman poured water from a pail onto the older woman's hands. "Goodness, I've never known equinox week to start out so hot! It feels good, though."

I'd heard of equinox week, with its traditional visits to the family graves. So far no one had died in our family, though, so I'd never given it a thought. She was right, it *was* hot.

I got to be very good at playing hooky, but going home still scared me to death every time. Turning into our side street gave me butterflies in my stomach, from expecting bad news. One day my mother was talking in front of our gate with Mr. Sawamura's mother from across the street. They stopped when they saw me coming. Mr. Sawamura taught art neither at Aoyama South nor at Yama, but at the more distant Saka Elementary School. When I got closer, I was relieved to find they were discussing a war that had broken out between Chinese and Japanese troops in Manchuria. Being such a coward, I'd mistaken their mention of Chô Sakurin (Chang Tso-lin) for talk about my *chômen*, my assignment book.

That evening my cousin, Jû-chan, turned up with stacks of newspaper extras and announced agitatedly, "That's it. I'm going abroad—France, England, Africa, anywhere." What he said gave me my first twinge of fear, but at the same time I couldn't stop laughing at the thought of a soldier with a fuzzy flannel wrap under his pants.

The cemetery being too dangerous during equinox week, I resigned myself to going to school and putting in my time standing. At the morning assembly the school principal talked about the war. It was rare for him to talk about anything unrelated to study or exams. Afterwards, when we returned to our classroom, the class president was sent to the teachers' office. A boy named Ôyama, whose father was in the army, volunteered to help. Then he brought in a helmet, an oiled paper umbrella, and a Chinese broadsword. These were booty his father had brought back from China and had now donated to the school. "Take a good look!" the teacher said and left the room. We immediately clustered around the podium. Saigô put on the helmet and picked up the sword. He carried on about how heavy it was. I wanted to try opening the umbrella, which Chinese soldiers apparently carried into battle in case of rain, but I decided not to. I knew I'd be blamed if it ever got broken. Those who couldn't get at the helmet or the sword gathered around Ôyama, who wore a military-style cap shaped with wire and, like a first-year student, kept a neatly folded handkerchief on his chest. His puckered little mouth kept prattling on gravely about something or other. I'd have hit him if he'd been alone.

What stopped me wasn't having to contend at the same time with so many others; it was something much more cheerful than that. The bell was ringing. The class president put the war booty back tidily on the teacher's desk. The teacher entered. I was sure he'd now tell us the story of how Ôyama's father had taken all this from some Chinese. Instead, however, he called the class president back again and had him take the things to the teachers' office. That kid—he must have just loved studying, he looked so pleased and proud. Meanwhile Mr. Kanehara, pickled radish odor and all, came around to make me stand.

It's raining. My raincoat's soaked. I've been squatting here for hours in a corner of the graveyard, on a thick pile of leaves. The rain keeps pouring down, and not a soul has been by all morning. I'm exhausted, I keep looking around to make sure nobody's coming up behind me, and when I lean against a big tree trunk to stretch out my legs, snails come pelting down onto them with the rain. I'm cold. For a moment I forget and stick my hands deep into my pockets, but then jerk them back out again. That half-baked appearance of mine at school now has me in a real pickle. I was about to take off home that day when the teacher handed me a letter. It's been right here in my pocket for three days. The first day, I really did forget to give it to my mother. Since then I've been too scared. The more crumpled the envelope gets, the clearer the letter's message is going to be. I'm cold, and it's getting dark, but I'm in no mood to go home. If only, I say to myself, I could stay like this forever! But suddenly, as I'm dreaming of somehow tracing the message, another temptation assails me. The envelope flap may come unglued if I moisten it just right. I can't wait to try. Why did I ever do it, anyway? I get up and go to look for some water. There isn't any, anywhere. All I can find is the water in a drainage ditch. Well, too bad. I crouch down and dip the envelope in the ditch. The soft brown paper blots up the water, and the ink runs. I've made a mess of it, but it's too late to be sorry. I drop the letter and shiver with cold as I pee into the ditch.

The first of October was the anniversary of the start of self-government for the city of Tokyo, and there was no school. My mother took me to visit a friend out in the suburbs. It was all the way on the other side of Setagaya-ku, and the ride on the Tamagawa Line took a long time. I was bored again after we got there. The lady assured me her son would be back any minute, but at the time I could hardly have cared less. I went to help a farmer dig potatoes in the neighboring field. It was actually rather fun, and the fine weather made treading the warm earth barefoot a pleasure. I dug away, determined to bring a great big one up from deep in the soil. Then it happened. Right there under the blue sky, I thought I was dreaming. I looked up, and there were four or five kids with their schoolbags, on their way home from school, peering at me through the hedge. I raced to the house next door. The son, just back from school, was standing there with his rucksack still on, staring suspiciously at me. His mother had a funny look on her face, too, as though she'd just remembered to wonder why I was here. *My* mother, however, had never even heard of this anniversary of Tokyo self-government. I'd told her there was no school that day, and she'd just believed me. In short, the vacation was only for schools within the city limits of Tokyo, like Aoyama South. Schools in places like Setagaya, outside the city, were holding classes as usual. Even so, that day never felt like a real holiday to me. It was a lot less relaxing than playing hooky.

After discarding the letter, I stayed well away from school. Still, I felt as though I really was going to school every day. Each morning I'd check the class schedule and set off with the appropriate books in my rucksack. I didn't run away or hide much any more. The lesson of equinox week had taught me not to fear being seen by people who didn't actually matter. Until about nine in the morning I'd make myself look like a kid hurrying to school because he's overslept and is late. After that, I'd be just getting over an illness and going to school in mid-morning. As a result, I thought about nothing but school. To tell the truth, I'd had enough of the graveyard. After a month of playing hooky, I was beginning to feel like someone who wants to go to school but can't, and so misses the place terribly. I'd toured the graves of General Nogi and all those other famous people, in the spirit of a kid on a school trip, but really they were no fun at all. Cutting through the graveyard, I found myself staring straight at the Yama Elementary School. I'd gathered that this one, unlike Aoyama South, practically never sent anyone on to the Tokyo metropolitan schools, but that it put its students into youth groups, taught them judo, and so on. Just then the school anthem blared from the three-story, reinforced concrete building. Gee! I exclaimed to myself, that's really great!

One day there was a festival at the local shrine near the Yama School, and I mingled with the Yama kids to go there. Boys and girls alike were dressed up in yellow and soft pink kimono, with white makeup on their faces. All were from Yama. They blew on whistling balloons, ate deep-fried skewered pork, and watched the monkey races and motorcycle stunt riding. Apart from the sideshows, there were also plenty of self-satisfied looking photographers, toy vendors, magicians, and so on. The man I'd bought the automatic pencil from was there, too. The Yama kids clustered around to listen to his spiel.

I couldn't resist boasting to one of them, "Well, *I've* got one of *those!*"

The pale, skinny kid looked at me in silence. He never answered me at all. I was a bit embarrassed—I'd probably come on too abruptly.

Then another kid who was staring at me from the side said, "You—you're from South, aren't you?" Next, I heard other voices nearby.

"South doesn't have off today!"

"If you're from South, go and play with kids from South!"

"You jerk!"

Before they could grab me I stuffed my cap inside my shirt, disappeared into the crowd, and left the shrine.

Was there *really* nowhere but the graveyard for me to hang out? I just couldn't take all those tombs any more. I thought back to the day when I'd first gone there to do my homework. I never did manage it. Anyway, I was behind the rest of the class in the first place, and I'd goofed off for a whole three months, counting the summer vacation, so what was the point of even trying? Decimals, fractions, the area of a circle—the thick book of math problems with its orange cover was gibberish to me. No, there was no chance that *I* was ever going to stand out. Still, I'd take being made to stand endlessly there over being alone in a cemetery. Right, I wanted to go into the advanced class. I'd heard those kids all became shop boys, but I'd be a lot better off that way than I was right now. Ôkuma or Piggy Suzuki might be willing to make friends with me. I'd tell the teacher the whole story about the letter.

The rain that had been falling that morning stopped, and the sun shone even on the gravestones. Brandishing my umbrella, I stopped off to buy some bread and then went to school.

Unlike Yama, the school building at South was old painted wood. Some of the windows were broken. This wasn't because the school was poor, though. The place was bursting with all the students packed into it. Its success in moving students on to higher schools had made it famous all over Tokyo, and a lot of kids came there by bus or train from outside the district. Yes, it was true, I'd take South over Yama.

It happened to be lunchtime. Walking along the corridor I could hear excited voices coming from the classrooms—all except for mine, which was dead silent. The instant I opened the door I regretted it. The teacher had the lid of my desk open and was showing off the contents to the class. Weeks ago I'd blown my nose and stuffed in there the crumpled hanky that he was now dangling, with a show of revulsion, from the very tips of his fingers. As though on cue, the whole class laughed. One by one, the teacher exhibited things like scraps of paper, pencil shavings, and bits of bread that I didn't remember at all. However, he said nothing bad about me personally. As far as he was concerned I didn't even exist any more, except as a lesson for the others. When the laughter stopped, the teacher turned round and saw me standing there in the doorway.

"What are *you* doing here?"

"I wanted to come back to school, sir, so I came. I had a stomachache."

I'd meant to tell the whole truth, but I managed to get out only the first half of it.

"No, you've been wandering around somewhere."

It made me mad, the way he seemed to know everything.

"I was in bed at home!"

The teacher burst out laughing. That square, boxlike jaw of his opened, and out came his front teeth.

"Turn around," he said. "Why, your whole backside's caked with mud! There's even mud on your ears!"

I fled, with the whole class of seventy or more hooting with laughter behind me. No, I'd never go back to that rotten school, never, never, never!

I was hardly out of the school gate when I heard behind me such shrieking as to rend the earth. Turning around, I saw a horde of kids coming after me, filling the width of the road. I was surrounded by cannibals and had no idea where to run. With desperate speed I raced to Mr. Shimazu's vacant lot. Diagonally across it I came up against the garden wall, and there I cowered, in a hollow under an evergreen tree. The enemy immediately encircled me.

"Come on out!"

"Come on out!"

Voices hailed me from a distance on three sides. Behind me was a stone wall. A huge drum seemed to be pounding away inside me. All right, they had me. So why didn't they try to grab me? In this battalion of truant-bashers I caught sight even of Piggy Suzuki, bawling away, hands to his mouth like a megaphone. I didn't want to go home. I didn't want my mother to see me like this, hunted down by the pack. There was no hope, though. They were going to kill me. I screwed up my courage, took off my rucksack, put it on my head, and broke through the besieging forces. Fortunately, there was no one home. I'd no sooner locked the gate behind me than the horde swept down like a tidal wave. I expected them to start climbing over the fence, but they didn't go that far. Through a crack between *shōji* paper doors on the second floor I watched them disperse by ones and twos, till at last I noticed the cold sweat running down my back.

My mother returned about two hours later.

That evening, my father was away on a business trip. Jû-chan came over, and the three of us were chatting after dinner when Mr. Sawamura turned up from across the street. He called my mother to the entrance, then they both went straight upstairs to talk. Mr. Sawamura usually came around to ask us to buy his paintings, so it was natural to assume that he had the same thing in mind this evening. After what had happened today, though, I pricked up my ears. The voices from the second floor sounded like the buzzing of flies, and I couldn't make out a word. I dropped my conversation with Jû-chan.

I don't know how long it had been, but suddenly Jû-chan looked at me and exclaimed, "How awful! Well, I'd better get home. Tell Auntie good-by for me." That was all. Then he practically ran from the house. How did Jû-chan know that something awful had happened? I was too frightened to go upstairs, but I couldn't stand being alone downstairs, either. At first I stole up silently, step by step, planning to eavesdrop; but then it was less impatience than fear of those two low voices that made me go straight up the dark, narrow stairs. My mother and Mr. Sawamura smiled when they heard me and saw me standing there.

"Where's Jû-chan?" my mother asked.

"He left a while ago."

My mother smiled even more sweetly. "Come here," she said. "Closer. How's school lately? Are you enjoying it?"

Mr. Sawamura had been back home from school, painting, when the day's uproar occurred. He'd gone straight to Mr. Kanehara when he heard what the children were shouting, and he passed Mr. Kanehara's account of my evil deeds on to my mother. "If he doesn't make a clean breast of it this evening," Mr. Sawamura had warned her, "he'll be a liar all his life." That was why my mother made such an effort to question me gently.

"Are you going to school every day?"

Not knowing what was happening, my only thought was to save my skin. "Of course I'm going, every day."

The next day I didn't know what to do. My mother made me lots of *norimaki* rolls for my lunch, just as she did for a school excursion. Perhaps that's why my rucksack was so terribly heavy that all I could see as I walked along was the ground. Suddenly I noticed that I'd passed the usual intersection and was heading straight for the cemetery. I had no wish to turn back. By now the cemetery smelled of dead grass. There were hardly any mosquitoes or other bugs left. I just sat around vacantly in the grass till afternoon, but the ground was cold, and I didn't feel like eating when I eventually got up. I followed my own footsteps, having nowhere special to go. In time I came out on a street I'd never been on before. On one side was a ditch and on the other a cemented embankment. Yellow handbills were pasted to the cement. I glanced at them.

STOP THE WAR!!! they said in fuzzy, mimeographed characters. NO MORE WAR!!!

What?? I took another look. The sheets were covered with tiny, closely packed writing. I hadn't the faintest idea what it was all about. Why would anyone be against war? I stretched up and tore off a corner. It felt like the times when you put rocks on the rails and watch from safely distant hiding to see what happens when the train goes by. I was seriously annoyed when the handbill didn't tear properly. I put down my rucksack, stood on it, and tore at the sheet with my nails, but it stuck firmly to the cement. What's wrong with war? Of course there have to be wars. I remembered what school was like the day the war began. The teacher was talking about joining the army if it went on. Fine! Go! All of you! Jû-chan, Mr. Kanehara, Mr. Sawamura, every one of you, go! Let Aoyama South burn! Bit by bit the handbill came off. There were three of them, pasted side by side. Moistening my fingers with saliva, I tore away at them without another thought in the world.

There are footsteps coming up behind me. Could it be a policeman? As always, I jump with fright, but then I change my mind and keep at it. It *is* a policeman. He looks at me and tells me what a good boy I am. He writes my name down in his book, and the next day the school principal praises me. This student tore down handbills that said bad things! Mr. Kanehara sticks out his teeth and smiles.

The footsteps fade away. I start in on the next handbill and go on dreaming. This student so honors the school that he is henceforth excused from all homework and allowed to sit comfortably in his classroom.

The House Guard

I had this crazy job a couple of years after the war. "House guard," it was called. It involved minding private houses requisitioned by the Allied Forces, whenever they were empty.

Most guards were students working part-time, like me. We were attached to the Services Section of GHQ; from there they sent us out to vacant houses all over Tokyo. With each assignment we received general and special orders, just like soldiers on guard duty. The general orders required us to protect the contents of the house from theft or fire, to handle foreigners who came looking for a house to rent, and to supervise maids and housekeepers. The special orders consisted of whatever injunction came to mind at the time, such as, "Prohibited: wearing only underwear," or "Prohibited: grilling fish and stinking up the house." In all there were several dozens of these orders, enough to put off any neophyte, and it was undoubtedly true that if you kept them all you'd never have a chance to sleep or even sit down. In reality, though, they were irrelevant, and as long as you didn't get caught you could safely ignore them all. Anyway, who could possibly keep an eye on someone all alone in a house?

The guard headquarters was in the GHQ building basement. M, the Japanese supervisor, spent his days there in endless agitation. Small even for a Japanese, and surrounded by gigantic American soldiers, M clung to his desk in a corner of the room in a permanent state of panic. He seemed to suspect his subordinates, who were all beyond his reach, of indulging at times in intolerable behavior.

Somehow or other, M just didn't seem to approve of me. The guys he liked, the smart ones, got sent to magnificent residences rented by generals and colonels. Those places had electric refrigerators, fans, pink porcelain bathroom fixtures—all the classy stuff you'd find in a fancy hotel. But me—one day I was called into the office to find M affecting a rather unnatural smile. "S is quitting," he said, "and I want you to replace him. The Russian officer who was living there set the place on fire, and half the house burned down, so I want you to watch out especially for fire."

Talk about depressing! Come to think of it, I'd heard a vague rumor of this Russian's half burned-down house. Apparently it had no electricity, and half the roof was gone. No wonder living in a place like that had been too much for S, however stoic he might be.

When I got there, feeling like an exile, the house turned out to be one of a cluster occupied by Russian Embassy personnel. Like other requisitioned houses it had a white, wooden sign on it bearing a US requisition order number, and the mere sight of the stone wall around it suggested damp and darkness. A red dog dashed up, barking, when I went in the gate. With a sigh I contemplated a two-story house, painted a light yellow. Soot from the fire had blackened the walls, and the second-floor windows gaped like inky caverns. Timidly I crept closer and peered in through the front window. The room was in surprisingly good shape. I saw a bed with a thick mattress on it, a desk, chairs, and a cabinet.

"Come on in!" S shouted when he saw me. "You're my replacement? You're in luck, believe me. This house is the greatest. Nice neighbors, too. I'd never give it up if school didn't demand so much of my time now."

S was right. There was only one room left after the fire, but, facing southeast as it did, it was bright and sunny, and it caught every breeze. The gas and water were on, and a cable—presumably the work of S, an engineering student—brought in electricity from a pole near the front garden. So I had it made.

Properly speaking, the business of guarding empty houses involved nothing that could be called work. In this case, nothing in the burned-out house was worth stealing anyway, and on top of that, foreigners hardly ever came around to fuss about one thing or another. There were no maids or houseboys to involve me in their endless, tedious quarrels. In a fine, big house, I'd have had to put up with inspectors' complaints if I didn't keep everything clean and tidy, but here, where no one had even cleared away the burnt wreckage, I could get away with being as sloppy as I liked, and if there happened to be a fire, nobody was going to accuse me of anything unless the whole building actually burned to the ground.

I tested the bed. The mattress wasn't too clean, but the springs made up for it. All the cooking pots, plates, and other such utensils that remained usable after the fire were stored in the cabinet along with army blankets for the bed. The flush toilet worked perfectly, and everything else necessary for comfort—desk, electric lamp, gas stove, and so on—was there as well. The only thing missing was a telephone, but that didn't bother me. If there had been one, the only calls I could have expected would have been from the frantic M in his underground office at GHQ, asking whether I was properly carrying out my special orders. There I'd be, sprawled naked on the bed, and I'd have to answer, "Yes, yes, I have my trousers on."

So there I was, earning rather more than a salaried worker fresh out of college, living rent-free in a house—half burnt-out or not—

equipped with all the modern conveniences, and spending my days ensconced in the depths of a great big easy chair (well, yes, it did have a broken leg). What an amazing job! I could lie there absently watching the hands move on the clock, and I'd still be making money. The idea made me feel pretty strange.

It was like when I was a kid playing hide-and-seek. I'd be waiting, holding my breath, in the depths of some dark closet, but whoever was "it" never came round at all, and suddenly I'd be scared to death that everyone had forgotten all about me. Generally speaking, being a house guard was just like playing hide-and-seek. "It" was the inspector, except that this one came by jeep. Night or day, he sniffed out negligence and checked your job performance, and when he caught you, it was "Gotcha!" and that's it, no excuses. If he found you at fault, you were fired, period. Most of the time, though, when you were violating one of those dozens of orders, the sound of his jeep inspired a surefire emergency way to fool him. Say you were eating from sealed utensils you weren't supposed to use: you just slid the plate and cups under the sofa. Or if you were sleeping on the bed you weren't supposed to sleep on, you just turned the mattress over.

As a matter of fact, no inspector ever came around to this half-burned Russian house.

I got horribly bored. It was an oddly deep-seated feeling I'd never experienced before. My isolation aroused the absurd suspicion that GHQ had forgotten all about me, till sometimes I actually missed M's constant nagging and came to long for the thrill of an inspection. On the other hand, I worried that having nothing to do for so long might make me stupid enough to blunder and lose my cushy job. The sound of a jeep crunching on the gravel at the gate always put me in the mood to mend my sloppy ways, and I'd peer out the window. A relief akin to despair came over me every time the lamplight out there showed it was marked not "USA—GHQ," but "USSR."

Becoming a house guard encouraged in me an interest in cooking, both for profit and as a pastime. After all, every house had a big, oven-equipped stove, as well as a gear-driven potato masher, an egg whisk, and other such gadgets. Fancy cuisine was no problem. However, the good fortune that had led me to this present house soon made it irrelevant, because every day the beautiful, kind maid from the Italians' house, catty-corner across the street, brought me more delicious food than I could eat.

I awoke every morning to her tapping on the window.

"Good morning!"

I'd open the window, and from under her apron she'd take apples and milk and cheese and boiled eggs that she'd line up on the windowsill. Then she'd take the dishes for the chicken and macaroni au gratin she'd given me the evening before.

"Was it good? Did you like it? I'll bring you some more at lunchtime." She'd laugh brightly and hurry away again.

At first I was a little nervous; her kindness seemed so excessive.

"Is it *really* all right for me to take all this?"

"Why do you ask?" she replied, eyes wide with surprise. She assured me it *was* all right, because her employer (a man with the same name as the great Garibaldi) had guests to dinner almost every evening, and the failure of some to turn up meant there was always food left over.

This sweet maid had just one shortcoming: she was terribly jealous. She'd go on and on about it if I didn't finish every scrap. "Why didn't you eat this?" she'd say. "I suppose my cooking's no good. There's bound to be someone better, somewhere." Then she'd turn her back on me. So, however stuffed, I had to lick every platter of Chako-chan's cooking clean. The business of eating came to feel like a kind of duty, and I shuddered at the very idea of cooking for myself.

I was so bored, I read a book titled *Pig Farming* and thought seriously about it. The shower room of this half-burned place was apparently ideal for a pigsty, and to feed the pigs I could get any quantity of rich leftovers from the foreigners' houses around. However, the thought of those inspections stopped me cold. It would be a grim day indeed if the GI who turned up to see how I was doing my job opened the door, and out popped a pig.

In Russian, *da* means "yes," *niet* means "no," and apparently *kaka* well and truly means "shit." Lena, the four year old daughter of Captain K, next door on the right, sometimes wet her pants while playing in the garden, and every time the Japanese maid looking after her would shout for the lady of the house. Her bellowing sounded as though she meant to place the blame where it belonged. "Oh no, no, no! What a child! There she's gone and soiled her pants *again*, without a word!" She might as well have been shouting, "This hopeless kid's *yours*, *you* gave to birth to her, so I'm yelling at *you!*"

Shrieking hysterically, the pale, skinny wife would come rushing out, rip off the girl's pants, and light into the maid.

"Kaka? NIET!!"

Maid and mother together would inspect the baby's bottom. "*What?*" the maid would answer in Japanese. "She didn't? She had this funny look on her face—I was sure she'd done it again!"

Watching this often-repeated scene taught me *da*, *niet*, and *kaka*; but otherwise, I who spent day after day without a thing in the world to do learned not one word of their language. Toward evening I sometimes heard Captain K's wife singing a lullaby to their newborn son. I didn't understand a word of the song, but her voice, richer even than a man's, reminded me of a cow mooing. Still, there was something Eastern about the tune, something more physically compatible with us, who so little resemble Americans and Europeans.

Actually, it's hard to explain why, but Russians really are more like us than Europeans or Americans. That's the feeling you get just seeing one—a sort of empathy. They're crude, and in our presence they swagger, but they're not overbearing like the Americans, the British, the Germans, and so on. Captain K's wife was like that. She was a slave driver, and the way she might put a napkin on the baby instead of a diaper had given her a bad reputation among all the maids of the neighborhood, but she was the only one who now and again cheerfully joined their back-fence gossip sessions.

Next door on the left lived Mr. Moskarev, who worked at the Russian Embassy. His reputation was more or less the opposite of Mrs. K's. People thought him a gentleman, and they were afraid of him. He was about my age, going on thirty, but he was a star graduate of the Japanese language program at Moscow University, and his Japanese was so good, reading *The Tale of Genji* was nothing for him. In fact, when he set off to work in the morning, sliding his lanky form into his car while his light spring coat flapped in the breeze, he looked every inch the lively, up-and-coming young diplomat. He usually got home late, around nine or ten at night. That was when they often did inspections, and I'd worry whenever I heard a jeep out front. I'd peer out through the curtains to make sure it was Moskarev's car. "US . . . aha, SR!" I'd say to myself with a sigh of relief when I read the letters on the side.

One day Shige-san, the Moskarevs' man-of-all-work, turned up at the door. The balding Shige-san looked old enough to be my father, but he was always reserved when he spoke to me. He usually cadged a smoke from me, too. While he fidgeted around I held out a packet of Shinsei cigarettes, but he waved it away. "I'm sorry," he said, "but the boss is angry. Why does the flunky in that house look through the window every time I come home? he says. I'm supposed to ask you not to."

"Oh," I answered vaguely, having no idea what this was all about.

"The boss is all right," he went on, "but he's awfully suspicious.

You'd hardly believe how much you worry him. He seems to think you're an American spy."

I burst out laughing, but Shige-san responded with a feeble, embarrassed smile.

"You *are* from GHQ, you know," he said.

I chortled again. Well, yes, it might look a little odd that I was lounging around all day in this half-burned wreck of a house as a so-called "guard." To Moskarev, my frightened eyes peering from the behind the curtains could easily look like those of a crafty watcher. Still, he really was taking it too far. For a spy, what could possibly be the point of watching him get out of his car whenever he came home—a spy who, on top of everything else, knew no more than "yes" and "no" of the "enemy language"?

"I see. All right, I get it. I'll stop."

While giving Shige-san this reassuring promise, I reflected with surprise that, from the outside, even *I* apparently looked smart enough to be Secret Agent Number XXX.

To tell the truth, my peering out the window had to do less with fear of inspectors than simply with habit. By this time, I hardly felt I was doing a job anymore. They say people can become accustomed to anything, however painful, and it certainly was no problem getting used to a life that provided me with housing, meals, and a fixed monthly salary. Was I just taking it too easy? Actually this house, with its roof more than half gone after the fire, was falling to pieces surprisingly fast. The floor and rafters were slowly rotting away, the gutters were falling off, and the plumbing pipes, no longer supported by the walls, rattled every time water passed through them. I took little notice of these daily changes. When a loud crash woke me up at night, I just thought, "Right, there goes another wall."

Whenever Mr. H, the owner, showed up, he'd look up at his disintegrating house and say, "I really should redo the roof, at least, right away." Then he'd lament the requisition regulations that prevented him, as long as they remained in force, from taking the initiative to repair his own property. Those were the only times I felt I might possibly be in danger of losing my job, but to make him feel better I answered the opposite of what I thought: "You're absolutely right. The government should fix it as soon as possible and then give it back to you."

Chako-chan, the maid, was looking forward to her approaching birthday. She'd get a present from her employer, Mr. Garibaldi, and she'd also have special time off.

"I'm not that happy about it, though," she said. "My parents and my brothers are all so far away!"

She'd come to Tokyo alone from Hokkaido.

"OK, why don't you come to my place? Not that I can offer you any entertainment, I'm afraid."

"Why, I'd love to!"

You couldn't tell that day whether it was her birthday or mine. She turned up, carrying a large bundle, in the morning when I was still in bed.

"It's awfully early, isn't it?"

"Yes, it is. There's no need to look cross about it, though. *I'm* the guest today! Anyway, here's breakfast."

She fed me the usual toast and fruit, then set about straightening the room. She put away everything that was dirty and polished the windows till they sparkled. Then she moved on to the kitchen. The rattling of pots and pans was quickly followed by delicious smells. I at least cleaned up the scorched paneling and plaster strewn around the bathroom, then heated the bath and had her go in first.

I emerged from my own bath to find both my room and Chako-chan herself only barely recognizable. She'd piled up the drawers from the cabinet, put a dazzlingly white, starched tablecloth over them, and turned them into a dining table. There wasn't a speck of dust on the floor, and the desk sported red and white roses in an empty whiskey bottle.

In no time, *hors d'oeuvres* were followed on the table by dish after dish worthy of a first-class restaurant.

"This is *amazing!*"

"Absolutely. I've been planning it for a week." She was wearing a brand-new, filmy dress with a flower pattern, and her abundant hair hung down to her shoulders. Even her nails shone.

"I just can't get over it!"

She chuckled. "Marry me, and this is what you'll get every day!"

We sat across from each other, napkins on our laps. The wine soon got to work, and the virginal stiffness vanished from her face. Her eyelashes glistened moistly, and a flush spread over her cheeks. I could see her breasts moving under the soft material of her dress. She put a record on the portable player she'd brought from next door.

"Won't you dance with me?" she asked and had just started to get up when we heard a jeep drive in through the gate.

"What's the matter?"

I'd apparently gone pale, to her surprise.

My heart was beating fast.

"It's nothing," I said, hoping to let the matter drop, but my eyes kept going to the window. Somewhat unsteadily, she went to it and peeked through the curtain.

"It's Mr. Moskarev."

There was a knock on the door. In fact, the battering was threatening to break it down. I ran to the entrance.

I opened the door to find looming before me in the night a dark, towering figure. In he came, as though to crush me.

"The other day," he said in a rich, strangely accented voice, "I believe you made Shige a promise. And just now you looked out the window."

I was going say no, it wasn't me, when I realized that if Chako had done it, I might as well have done it myself. So I answered, "That's right."

Then he really let me have it. Belting me hard in the chest, he seized my collar and practically strangled me with it.

"Why you lie? I no Chinaman. I Russian. You no lie to me."

"OK."

His gray eyes and blond mustache were so close I could practically see every pore.

"You ever look again," he roared, "I bring soldiers from the embassy, they make mincemeat of you! You got that?" He slammed the door almost in my face, so hard that it recoiled and banged wide open again. Terrified, I hastened to shut it properly.

When I returned to my room, Chako-chan was gone without a trace. She must have been scared enough to slip out the back. In the dead silence, all those shamelessly soiled plates on the table filled me with loneliness and despair.

Gone was the elation of a few moments before. The merry dining table now looked like no more than a stack of upside-down cabinet drawers, and my face, burning with fear and amazement, began to cool off again. Then the things the Russian had just said and done returned to mind, sharper than ever.

"Next time you look, you're mincemeat! You got that?" These words, at once frightening and comical, struck me as an intolerable insult. I couldn't fight him, though. I could only let the feeling eat further and further into me.

The next day, the boredom of my former life gave way to something far worse, far more stiflingly dreary. Hopelessly lazy though I was, even I could no longer stand being shut up in a building that was falling apart around me day by day; but I still didn't have it in me to quit this job and find another. With idleness giving me no outlet for what energy I had, I seemed to be sinking to the depths of an unresisting bog that made it impossible to rise.

It was horribly depressing after that incident just to see Chako-chan's face, and I refused everything she brought me each morning.

Apparently she just gave up, because she didn't come around any more, either. I felt sorry for her, but the memory of that evening was too unbearable, and I could do nothing about it. Actually, it wasn't just that evening. Everything I'd been doing all this time, absolutely everything, was vaguely grubby. I drew back from Shige-san, from Mr. H the owner, and from everyone else as well, and when Mr. H started in on his usual complaints, I made it my practice to tell him bluntly what I really thought.

"You want at least to fix the roof? Well, it's no use talking to *me* about it! Go and ask the man in charge."

No doubt this was just what M the supervisor, in his basement GHQ office, would have wanted.

Jingle Bells

It was almost dark when the call from Mitsuko woke me. I'd been playing bad mahjong—three hours per game—continuously since the evening before, and I'd gone to bed just before noon.

"I'll be waiting for you at the Mitsukoshi-mae subway station. At five. OK?"

"Uh-huh. But I'm going to have to eat something. From here, it'll take me about an hour."

"All right, I'll wait thirty minutes. After 5:30, though, I'm gone."

"Yeah, yeah."

"I mean it!"

"Right."

In the half-light of the room, I could hardly tell whether it was dawn or dusk. I dithered for a moment, then the phone went dead.

From the moment I put the receiver down, I was strangely obsessed by food. I wasn't hungry, but the only thing awake in me was the idea of eating. Everything else was asleep.

I set out. For a winter day, it was nice and warm. I noticed when I got to Tamagawa-en station how mechanically my legs were moving.

"Jingle Bells" was playing on the radio, and I was walking in time to it. It was Christmas Day. Nonetheless, the eateries lining both sides of the street in front of the station were flying big red-and-white banners against the leaden sky, advertising "Grilled Sweetfish! Tamagawa Specialty! Tasty! Tasty!"

Jingle bells, jingle bells.

I tried *not* to walk in step, but it didn't work. I seemed to have cords around my ankles that kept me marching along. I remembered how in my first year as a member of the Takasaki Infantry Regiment the sergeant had called "Hup, two, three, four." The call came at every gap in the rhythm.

Jingle (hup) bells (two), jingle (three) bells (four). Feet slaves to the tune, I lurched into one of the grubby little shops, plopped into a chair and called out, "*Unadon!*"

Afterwards, I could never understand why. When the bowl of rice topped by grilled eel finally arrived, I took another look at the waitress. Whose order was this? I've always stayed away from eel. Army life had taught me not to be picky about my food, but I'd never eaten either eel or eggplant. Just as the photographer's black hood had scared me when I was a boy, I'd always been afraid of dark-colored foods. Eel in particular seemed creepy. Its flabby moistness made it hard to tell just what to do with it. I'd just as soon eat a couple of slugs at once, as eat an eel. Still, my memory assured me that I really had uttered the word "*unadon.*" I resolved to eat it; or, rather, for some reason I couldn't fight it. Encouraged by the two slices of pickled radish in the little dish beside the bowl, I picked up the chopsticks and ate one. Then I poked at the eel skin, grilled a dark reddish-brown. Underneath, it was a slippery, oily gray that slid aside to reveal the white, squishy flesh. This was where I'd normally quit in disgust, but this time I stuffed it straight into my mouth and gulped it down. Right then, I thought I heard my death rattle. Then another swallow. It's good for you, good for you, vitamins, vitamins, I repeated to myself like a prayer, meanwhile chewing away.

At last I got through it and asked what I owed.

"Three hundred yen," the waitress said, as though it was the most natural thing in the world.

I *had* known that eel is relatively expensive, but even so the price was a cruel blow after what I'd been through. I wanted at least a cup of hot tea, but I decided I'd better not ask for any extras. I paid my money and left.

The station clock said it was already 4:45. She'd said she'd wait half an hour, but I doubted I could get to Nihonbashi in forty minutes. Maybe I should just go home. Mitsuko would undoubtedly give me an impatient phone call if she couldn't wait any more. Then I'd be able to explain what had happened and apologize. That should do.

But then, there I was nonetheless on a Shibuya-bound train. It seemed to be rather late, and the train was packed. More people got on at Denenchôfu and Jiyûgaoka, but no one got off. I was squashed into a corner by the driver's cabin and could hardly breathe. My back got cold. Ah, here it is again! I thought, remembering the slight fever I'd been running. Last year, while writing my graduation thesis, I'd had a relapse of pleurisy, and recently again I'd been running a slight fever late in the day. "You'll die if you go on like this!" Mitsuko warned, and she allowed me only the lightest kisses. Nonetheless, when we went into town together she bought piles of things for herself and made me carry them: long underwear, yarn, a nutcracker, hair clips, things for making ice cream . . .

A little while after leaving Toritsu Kôkô Station, the train stopped dead. The sudden halt made the mass of passengers sway violently, but the train was so crowded that it then became impossible to move at all. Amid the press of people my face burned and sweat trickled down inside my long woolen underwear. The man opposite me had a black mask over his mouth and was wearing an absurdly large deerstalker hat, the brim of which came right to my eyes. For some reason he kept shaking his head from side to side, and every time he did, the brim practically poked me in the eye. I wanted to ask him to take it off, but there didn't seem to be much point in that, either. Anyway, he seemed to be trying to wriggle his hand out of the crush, so as to take his mask off. When at last he succeeded, he managed to slide his mask down to his chin by running his nose up my chest; but at the same instant his hat slipped off his head. The crisp, brown-checked deerstalker now rested on his shoulder. He kept twisting his short, fat neck around to train an anxious eye on it, but there was absolutely nothing he could do. Then he turned his resigned gaze to me. I felt a degree of sympathy for him. The area around his mouth was red from having stewed behind his mask, and drops of sweat gleamed at the end of his nose and on his sparse whiskers. Then, suddenly, it started up again.

Jingle bells, jingle bells . . .

Passengers had been opening windows here and there to let in some air, and presumably that infectious rhythm was coming from the radio in a coffee shop somewhere. Something weird was going on in my stomach. It felt hot, and my heart started beating strangely fast. *Jingle bells, jingle bells, jingle all the way . . .* With every *jingle* I felt that eel I'd eaten slithering back up my esophagus, and I felt sick. My ears began ringing the way they did up in the mountains, among the clouds, and my mouth filled with a steady stream of saliva. Desperate at all costs to breathe better air, I turned my face upward like a fish and tried sucking some in, but the ringing in my ears and the discomfort in my stomach didn't improve. There was nothing more I could do, except wait for the train to get under way again and bring some fresh air in through the windows.

Jingle bells, jingle bells . . .

So when *was* the train going to start moving? And how long was I going to have to listen to that confounded song? All I could do was stare past all those heads into the darkness outside.

By the time the train reached Shibuya I was exhausted. It was already past six, and it would be at least seven by the time I made it to Mitsukoshi-mae. Mitsuko would hardly wait two hours in a place where you couldn't even sit down. Undaunted, I set straight off down the platform toward the subway. It wasn't easy getting up the stairs to the subway. I had the tune on the brain now, and I hummed it at each step till I ran out of breath and staggered on like a drunk.

The train was just about to leave. I ran. I was so out of breath by the time I reached the top step that my head went blank. I threw myself into the car, and the doors closing behind me slid across my back. The train pulled out.

I leaned back against the doors and stared vacantly at the tunnel wall. My ears began ringing again. My overcoat weighed heavily on my shoulders. I remembered playing basketball in middle school. The four other members of a team always made a wry face when they realized I was the fifth. At the starting whistle, I'd begin racing around and around the court. Terrified that the ball might actually come my way, I'd wave my arms at random in all directions, shouting "All right! All right!" and charging blindly around. You couldn't just stand there. You had to keep running that way, pale-faced, till the period was over. The thing was a total waste of time. When I got to my station, there'd be nothing there. Still, I had to go. The goal was going, not getting there. Such were my thoughts while I watched the stations pass. But surprise, surprise! Lucky me! When the train reached Kyôbashi, it too broke down and was unable to go on. This was no trifling malfunction, either. They announced that it would not be fixed till the next day.

This was perfect. I started walking. The streetcars were running, but I was in no mood to wait for one. It was a pleasure after all to pass Nihonbashi and see the lights of Mitsukoshi-mae Station finally come into view. Seven-thirty—I felt like a marathon runner reaching the finish line. The station was empty, and naturally there was no sign of Mitsuko. A chain closed off access to the platform. Half a dozen people were lined up at the ticket booth to receive new tickets. I joined them. The stamp on my new ticket said it was valid for a week, in other words, till the end of the year, but it might as well have been no good, since the subway was useless to me on the way home. I'd done all I could. I stuck the ticket in my pocket and was starting for the exit again when I noticed the thickness of the station pillars. It would take two adults to reach around them. I turned back and had a look at each. To my surprise, a woman was standing by the one furthest from the exit. Her clothing suggested she was neither a station employee nor a Mitsukoshi Department Store clerk. She was facing the wall, but she turned round when she heard my footsteps. She was ugly.

There wasn't a soul to be seen along Nihonbashi Avenue on Christmas night. The darkened buildings towered blackly, an autumnal fog closed in, and the temperature was oddly warm. I'd given up, no doubt about it. Just one open fruit shop had its lights on. At the sight I felt I was saved. On further reflection, however, I had no idea what to do there. I turned to leave again but just couldn't.

"Give me 300 yen worth of those tangerines," I said at last, timorous as a rabbit run to ground by a hunter. I was thinking of the eel I'd eaten on the way. This time, however, the pile of tangerines heaped on the scales far surpassed anything I'd imagined. It was simply enormous. I wanted to beg the fruit man to make it a bit smaller, but he never gave me the chance.

One streetcar went by after another, but none was going further than Nihonbashi. I had to get on one and then walk to Tokyo Station. When I carried the bag of tangerines with one hand it crackled, and the tangerines threatened to burst out and roll all over the road, so I had to hold it tight against my chest. Then I could feel my heartbeat through the tangerines.

Eventually I passed what were presumably some clubs and cabarets. Through a glass window I saw a Christmas tree standing in an empty room. Three waiters in white coats and paper hats were stationed on the stone steps at the entrance. They were playing with party favors that shot out about a foot when you blew into them.

Jingle bells, jingle bells.

Suddenly, there it was again, coming through a loudspeaker set up so you could hear the band from the street. I quickened my pace, as though fleeing a pursuer, but the sound stuck stubbornly with me. It was a jazz version. The man singing it was obviously imitating some black singer.

JINgle BElls, JINgle BElls, JINgle, JINgle, huh, huh, huh, huh, huh, huh . . .

The voice was breathless, strangled, the phrasing like sobs and groans—perfect for a people born into slavery. I pictured a birch forest, a despairingly endless waste of snow, a sleigh dashing madly across it.

Jingle those bells, keep 'em jinglin', jinglin' . . .

A whip lashes down from the sleigh, again and again. On and on the reindeer must race, till their legs fail beneath them, till they drop.

Clasping the tangerines to my heart, I drove my tired legs on faster. I could hardly feel them any more.

The next day.

Rain.

I went to Mr. M's house in Shimo-Meguro to ask him to help my father find work. I took him some eggs our hens had laid, wrapped in newspaper. I envied my father. Formerly in the army, he'd been working in his garden ever since he was dropped from his post, dreaming only of growing nine-pound sweet potatoes. He seemed to have lost all interest in anything else. My mother wanted him to find a job, but whenever she got after him about it, he'd put on the beret I'd worn since I was a kid, assume an air of tongue-tied innocence, and say, "Ah, it's so nice, when you're an old man and you can wear a padded red vest!"

I wished my father would make it clear that he'd really given up hope. It did something to me to see my father wandering around the dug-up lawn with a shovel over his shoulder and that beret, spattered with bird droppings, on his head. What that thing was I couldn't say, though. Our family of three survived exclusively by selling our few remaining furnishings and utensils. It's not that I especially wanted my father to earn money. I couldn't criticize the way my father lived, but at the same time, I just couldn't stand it. My father took one of his old business cards when I said I'd talk to M for him, and he wrote on it a few words to introduce me.

M was out. I gathered he'd be home in about an hour. I went back to Meguro Station and was wondering what to do with the time I had on my hands when I noticed a public phone. Perfect! I hadn't called Mitsuko yet about yesterday.

At times like that things go amazingly smoothly. Mitsuko answered right away.

"Yesterday evening . . ." I began, but Mitsuko interrupted.

"You couldn't make it because the subway broke down, right?"

"Right. Well, actually, my Tôyoko Line train was over an hour late, too."

"I waited for you till after seven. Then they said a train had broken down, so I decided you weren't coming. After that everything went way off track."

"Off track?"

"Exactly. You weren't coming, right? I just kept smoking cigarettes to pass the time. When I gave up and started home, this man came up behind me. I *did* think he looked a bit strange."

The man had fed her a standard line. "Pardon me, Miss," he'd said, "but I believe the person you were waiting for failed to arrive. Actually, I myself . . ." Being so out of it by then, Mitsuko had gone along with him. She named a series of dance halls and coffee shops.

"I drank an awful lot of saké," she went on. "I completely lost track of what was happening, and I didn't get home till midnight."

For some reason I was relieved. It was the pleasure of feeling I'd somehow known it all along.

"You really shouldn't do things like that."

"It's your fault, though, you have to admit. How about coming over? No one's home. I've made some ice cream. Come on!"

"I can't. There's something I have to do."

"You're sure? This evening, then. This evening's OK, right? I'll put the ice cream in the freezer."

I hung up, left the phone booth, and suddenly began feeling pretty unhappy. The meaning of what she'd said was only now sinking in: she'd betrayed me. Amid the rising flames of anger, this effort to find my father a job looked like pure nonsense. Ice cream, hell! I started back to Meguro Station, planning to go straight to Mitsuko's house, and imagining myself mashing that ice cream of hers right down on her head.

But then, I could hardly believe my ears: it was "Jingle Bells" again. For pity's sake! Christmas was *yesterday*, wasn't it? Wasn't it over *yet*?

My gait fell again into *Hup, two, three, four*. I fought grimly to resist the rhythm that had mastered me yesterday, but I failed. Two or three steps in the rain, and I could hear it again: *Hup, two, three, four*. I limped, but that only made it worse. I forced myself to break the rhythm, but I hit every *Jingle* on my left foot, every *bells* on my right. There was no hope.

Jingle bells, jingle bells, jingle all the way . . .

It overwhelmed me with sadness to be driven to all this meaningless activity, this empty running around. Dazed, I leaned against the footbridge over the tracks and gave myself up to the melancholy lurking behind that jaunty rhythm. And this is what I felt like saying.

"Old Saint Nick, I can't keep up with you. I'm one of the reindeer hitched to your sleigh. I won't dawdle about just to suit myself, I promise you that, but please, just give me a minute to catch my breath!"

The King's Ears

This story is about how I suddenly realized I'd been had.

A few months before Toyota Fukumitsu (listed as missing in action) entered the army, he told me you could buy coffee at a store in Yokohama.

An Italian grocery called Hetora, near Yato Bridge in Yokohama, sold coffee. Mocha or Guatemalan, they had beans of all kinds and were glad to sell you whatever you liked. Toyota heard this from a Russian girl he met on a train on his way into the city to take his induction exam, and he passed the tip on to me in a letter. In those days, coffee had for me the same sort of mystical aura as the word "art," and I rushed straight there. The Yato Bridge he'd mentioned was right next to the New Grand Hotel. There were several big foreign-run stores in the area, and I was sure I'd find coffee somewhere. I found no trace of any Hetora, though, despite wandering around the hotel a number of times, and I went home empty-handed. After that I'd comb the area again whenever I had a chance, but I never tracked down the store Toyota had mentioned.

That was in 1941, and we were preparatory course students at a private university in Tokyo. Actually, it's only recently, during the years illness kept me confined to my bed, that I realized Toyota had just invented the whole thing. Why has that memory popped up again now, I wonder? Or, rather, why did it take me so long to catch onto so simple a tall tale? I suppose it's because I'm still seething over another of Toyota's malicious lies.

Till then, I myself had told Toyota nothing but lies. I really enjoyed the look on his face when he realized he'd been had. Dark-complexioned and square in face and build, like a suitcase that has sprouted arms and legs, every time I got him he rolled up his eyes and silently stroked his long, square chin with an expression that never failed to delight me, however often I did it. The biggest trick of all that I played on him, though, was when he didn't know which entrance exam to take for the university preparatory course, and I made him join me in opting for liberal arts.

A field of study was life itself for those of us who were preparing to take the exam. Going out for medicine meant you'd be reborn as a physician; choosing commerce meant you'd be a businessman. To go for liberal arts meant becoming that vague, mysterious entity, a "liberal arts type"—the kind of person who in all likelihood would never successfully occupy any particular position in society, and who in the end would just vanish in a puff of smoke. However, tempted by vanity, a spirit of adventurousness, and, most importantly, sheer sloth, I pretended to my parents that I was going to decide between economics and engineering, and actually went for liberal arts. Toyota was in the same situation. The only difference was that he was less adventurous than me.

"Am I going to be OK?" he kept asking anxiously.

"Of course you are. You've got talent."

Actually, though, the opposite answer came first to my lips whenever I said that. I knew I'd made a risky decision, and my chest tightened in anguish at the thought of undertaking such a perilous venture alone.

"Is it going to be OK?" he asked again, as though divining my thoughts. "Tell me the truth. Don't hide anything." He wanted to hear me repeat my vapid, "Of course you'll be OK."

At the time I didn't think I was actually deceiving Toyota. Both of us, I believed, were groping for something that we couldn't possibly understand; so when he asked me whether he had any talent or not, and I assured him that he did, I just felt it was important not to injure his self-esteem. In reality, I was quibbling in order to fool my own conscience. In the back of my mind I was just delighted to see the acutely anxious Toyota reveal his feelings to me this way and beg to be saved, but I didn't realize this for a long time. I experienced it as a sort guilt that I myself didn't understand. This guilt, lurking unseen like a disease, erupted now and again in small, threatening pimples and rashes.

I went to visit Toyota one day, a month after we'd registered at a liberal arts school, to find an ill-complexioned man in horn-rimmed glasses sitting alone in Toyota's cane chair, eating a bowl of prawn tempura over rice. Toyota noticed my expression and introduced him somewhat stiffly.

"This is Mr. Nakaya," he said. "He's my teacher."

"Your teacher?" I exclaimed in surprise.

An uncle of Toyota's was an up-and-coming Western-style painter, and Toyota had nothing but affectionate respect for him. Whenever this uncle got one of his works into an exhibition or won a prize, Toyota would announce to his friends, bashfully but with obvious pride, "This time Uncle Takasuke's gone and picked up the XXX Prize—he'll have a swelled head for sure, at this rate." Apparently Nakaya was an art critic friend of Uncle Takasuke. I had no idea what was going on. Toyota explained that Nakaya came once a week to teach him about music, painting, literature, and art in general, but I couldn't see what this skinny fellow with a food bowl on his lap, smacking his lips now and again as he brought the rice up to a mouth as red as pickled ginger, could possibly have to do with "art in general." Did Toyota really think he could learn anything from him, the way a poor student gets a tutor to help him with his algebra and his English homework? Before my eyes Toyota's broad face, with its bulging forehead and darting eyes, began to look like a sickly child's, and I grasped at last that I'd led him astray. At the same time, my suspicion that Nakaya was the epitome of the vaguely conceived "liberal arts type" gave me the uncomfortable feeling of seeing in him our own future.

That day Nakaya finished his meal and left without a word, leaving behind on the table only a brownish, grubby book. Apparently I hadn't impressed *him* favorably, either, since I learned later on that Uncle Takasuke had given Toyota a warning. "Nakaya tells me you have an undesirable friend. You'd better look out," he said.

However, Toyota soon parted company with this tutor of his. Instead, he and I both joined a bunch that called themselves the Loonies. They affected an indescribably peculiar style of dress that included wearing a student cap minus its bill for a beret, together with a high-collar jacket; a stiff sash over a filthy silk kimono; or even an old-fashioned aesthete's cap with army surplus cavalry boots. All of them were more or less our own age. In these bizarre outfits we'd parade through Asakusa, Ryôgoku, or Tsukiji, commenting on the people lined up in front of restaurants and theaters.

"The Japanese really love standing around in queues, don't they."

Late at night, gazing out over the river from Sumida Park, we'd remark, "'States fall, mountains and rivers remain.' Only mountains and rivers remain aloof from the culture of the new order." We resisted the cult of airmen and naval officers, opposed the ideas of control, rules, and order, and rejected everything "new." Under this banner we spent our entire time amusing ourselves.

None of us had the slightest idea what to do with ourselves. Our professors, already caught up in their own dread of the times, devoted their Japanese history classes to nonsense like having us read *Mein Kampf* aloud, or to other such absurd, perfunctory tasks, so that for us school was a place you went to only to earn credits. Toyota had orders from his uncle, the up-and-coming painter, to take the first step toward becoming an artist by visiting the museum at Ueno twice a month, but in such a setting he registered only the reflections in the glass of the exhibition cases, having neither the patience nor the fortitude quietly to contemplate the objects displayed within them. We of the Loonies, always against whatever showed up in front of our noses, at any rate had an immediate motive to do *something*, and our combined inexperience and faintheartedness turned the slightest gesture into an inspiring adventure. For example, we'd set off to drop a bomb in the street, as we called it, by trooping in our outlandish garb into a first-class restaurant, banging our forks on our plates, rattling our chairs, eating macaroni with our fingers, splashing sauce all over the tablecloth, and bringing a frown to the face of every patron around us before we left. At such times the slightest vacillation would finish us. The glares of the chefs and waiters would terrorize us, and we couldn't swallow a thing. Each of us therefore went all-out to keep up with the rest in making as much uproar as we could.

After about three months of that, though, we began to feel weighed down by an indescribable burden. Despite our ambition to shake off every restraint, we seemed to have been trapped by some sort of invisible flypaper. Constraint sprang up between us, within the group. One time I spent the night roaming with the others through the area on the other side of the Sumida River, to end up sneaking into the Asakusa Review theater, which opened its doors in the early morning, and spending several hours there asleep in the seats, clutching bread rolls and bottles of lemon soda. Later, strolling down sunny Rokku Avenue, we ran into a group of three or four girls, all about the same age and apparently dancers somewhere.

They gave us the once-over together, which I'd no sooner spotted than they walked right by us, eyes to the ground, poking each other's bottoms. Perhaps it was the way they were dressed, all in vivid red and yellow, that gave me a headache.

"Too bad!"

"We should've run after them!"

That was their talk as they walked beside me, but to me it sounded completely fake. I could think of nothing but the unspeakably miserable spectacle we were making of ourselves, even in this motley part of town.

Just one incident like that, and afterwards everything we got up to looked stupid. For example, the others heaped ridicule on Toyota and me when we happened now and again to wear our school uniform, but I came to realize that they did it out of spite at no longer being registered students themselves.

However, even as I began to feel that way, I was in a tight spot myself.

I had no idea what I was doing. I couldn't figure out why Mr. Nakaya had decided Toyota should beware of me, but what he'd said worked on us both like a soothsayer's prophecy. Whenever we were together, I had the feeling that he was suspicious of me. I'd glance at his face after making some remark, and it seemed to me that in the depths of his big, dull eyes he was saying, Tell me another! Surprisingly enough, I noticed whenever this notion crossed my mind that every remark of mine *had* been a fib. I fully recognize now that I had indeed led Toyota astray, but I couldn't confess this openly to him, so I tried to make up for it by, for example, allowing myself be taken in by my own lies. Toyota, on the other hand, had his own perspective on me. He'd already given up asking me his plaintive question, "Is it going to be OK?" Instead, he tried to go me one better at everything. Cultivating as he did a feeling of superiority, he took the way I scrutinized his expression, in fear of my own lies, for obnoxiously honeyed fawning on him. As a result, the harder I tried not to lie, the more massively I deceived him. Whether or not I could back out of the Loonies depended, too, on how I meshed with Toyota, because for me to leave the group on my own would amount to tricking him yet again, while to get him to drop out with me, I'd need to steer him in that direction. In short, I was stymied by his deep suspicion of everything I did.

We no longer went to school, but we spent no time at home; by this time the Loonies had taken over our lives. Toyota and I, though, seemed to have joined them only to be their victims. We'd always met most of the expenses for the group's adventures, and it's not just that the amount required kept growing; they made us keep doing precisely the things we were the least good at and disliked the most. Our demonstrations in restaurants, for example—now that I think about it, I suspect they enjoyed watching Toyota and me pale with embarrassment even more than they did tormenting the waiters and the patrons. Considering the two of us girlish in our ways, they'd make a point of doing to us things that no one could help objecting to. Once when Toyota had on a pair of white tennis slacks, freshly washed, they cooked up an excuse to make him sit on a roof covered in wet paint. Whatever they did, we couldn't fight it. In the Loonies spirit they really did do exactly as they pleased, and we could only go along with it.

Then some things happened that we just couldn't take. One of the guys wanted to borrow money from me, so I took off my watch and gave it to him. Four or five days later, there he was, wearing my watch.

"I can't eat properly without it," he said. He claimed he had to have it because he took his meals at an eatery that served food only at fixed times. At about the same time, Toyota got it even worse.

The club leader, a fellow named M, caught gonorrhea. Someone was going to have to pay his medical expenses.

"I . . ." Toyota began.

"You will?" M replied. "Thanks a lot. But I want you to make out that you're the one who's got it. Have the doctor make his bills out in your name, and just take them to your parents."

Toyota and I were stretched out on the grass of a park overlooking the port of Yokohama. That morning I'd gotten on the train to school, after a long absence, and there in the seat in front of me was Toyota. We'd let the school's station go by, and since then we'd just been killing time. It was ages since we'd done anything like that together.

For a good while we just watched, without a word, a great ocean liner moored idly at a pier. Then I suddenly realized that friendship was right here before my eyes. Just as roiled water slowly clears again, in Toyota's silent presence I felt as though the Toyota I'd known before our relationship turned prickly was lying there beside me.

I really had no premonition of any danger. We discussed the ship's speed and navigational ability just as though we were middle school students again.

Talk of the price of a ticket inspired me to remark, "Not that long ago, you'd have been able to save up a thousand yen, then go to France and live there a whole year on it." On the basis of novels and travel accounts I'd read, I worked out an imaginary budget listing the cost of transportation, lodging, meals, and even laundry. "OK, so there's three yen left over in change. You take that to Monaco and gamble it at a hundred to one. If you win, you can spend another year in France and get the same three yen back at the end."

I wrote all the expenses down in great detail on a piece of notepaper, just as though I'd been recording mahjong scores. Then, for some reason, our conversation jumped to the topic of joining the army. It was like when a girl leafing through a fashion magazine dreams first of evening gowns, then suddenly shifts to considering what kind of apron to wear in the kitchen. We couldn't go overseas because we hadn't yet undergone our induction exams, and if we did want to travel beyond Japan to see other lands, the quickest way to do it was to enter the army. The way our conversation darted from topic to topic made it hard for me to believe that it concealed any ill will on his part. I felt only a tense sort of romance in this attempt to link our happiest but least realizable dreams with our dreariest but most plausible imaginings.

At any rate, the army stood before us like a wall that cut off our future and repulsed whatever fantasies we cared to entertain; so that if we wanted to embellish a little what lay before us in life, all we could do was embellish the way we thought of the army.

Starting from the resemblance between the Japanese army service cap, with its neck flap to protect the wearer from the sun, and the cap worn by the French Foreign Legion, then moving on item by item to bugles, banners, pistols, and so on, we managed in our enthusiasm to fantasize an army worthy of a children's story.

"Let's just do it!" I exclaimed. "Look, we're not doing ourselves any good just dragging around this way!" I didn't feel right about not going to school, and I thought that once I was back from the army I could settle down to studying. "At school these days all they do is mimic the army, anyway," I went on. "I can't stand it."

"That's right," he said. "There's always more beauty in the real thing. If the choice is between school and the army, then the army's the one to go for."

We talked on until darkness began to spread over the sea, and we promised each other that the very next day we'd begin the process of enlisting. I had a strange sense of liberation.

The next morning, for some reason, I overslept till almost noon. I hadn't gone to bed that late the evening before, but by the time I woke up it was too late for my promised rendezvous with Toyota. Toyota went to the recruitment office alone, then came all the way to my place to let me know what the formalities were and how the deadline for voluntary enlistment wasn't that many days away.

"The girl at the reception desk is a real looker," he said. "You'd better get over there."

"Really? All right, I'll do that before you get too far ahead of me."

It was strange, during those ten days leading up to the deadline, how even I hated to imagine what I'd done. Over that period I saw Toyota four times. The second time he came was two days after the first. He told me his uncle Takasuke, the painter, had praised our resolve and assured him that we had a bright future ahead of us if we went through with it. What he said reminded me that I, too, would do well to discuss my decision with someone. For the purpose I selected Colonel K, an army friend of my father's. Colonel K had once called at the same recruitment office, on an errand of my father's, and he'd taken the opportunity to treat me to a meal at a famous French restaurant nearby. I thought back to that meal as I set off. All I really wanted was to taste that soup again. He was a military man, after all—he would hardly oppose my plan. It's true, though, that my calculations in the matter were a little complicated. Mindless as I was, I'd figured that, despite being a military man, Colonel K also prided himself on his worldly *savoir faire*. No doubt I assumed pessimistically that if he didn't like the idea I wouldn't get any soup.

Sure enough, K was against it. He seemed to enjoy quelling the mounting wave of blind, youthful patriotism. For me, that was perfect. I eagerly kept the argument, which I was sure to lose, going for over an hour and as a result scored a large box of buns filled with bean jam and some sort of greens, freshly made by the Army Quartermaster Corps.

The third time I met Toyota, I fed him some of my buns, told him how discouraged I was, and explained why. For a second a shadow passed over Toyota's face, but then he laughed merrily. I suppose he hadn't expected what Colonel K said to sway me. I could only try to persuade him that it hadn't.

The fourth time I saw Toyota was the day before the deadline. We met in a run-down coffee shop on a Ginza back street. I'd often gone there with him and the others when I went out in the evening. I went up to the second floor. What with the growing difficulty of obtaining foodstuffs the place was already quiet enough in those days, but this time it was like a tomb. I was the only one there. I sat in a corner. The light outside the glass windows, with their tatty, grubby curtains; seemed for a moment to dim altogether. Just then, I caught Toyota's reflection as he came up the stairs on the opposite side. I'll never forget his expression. The eyes in his ashen skin looked as though they opened onto a watery void. He seemed not to realize that the only patron on the second floor was me, and he began cruising among the tables on his long legs as though he were swimming. I heard myself hail him.

"Toyota!"

"Oh, *there* you are, are you?"

That was when I knew I wanted to get out of there.

"How'd it go? Did you get through all the formalities?" His face was the picture of innocence.

"No, not yet." I hadn't yet gotten together my family register and all the other documents I'd need. I wasn't going to make it in time for tomorrow.

Toyota showed no particular sign of blaming me. In his eyes I'd betrayed him, but in the very moment when I'd done him in all the way, he himself had seen right through my heart, which he'd been out to test. Soon after that he left for his parents' home city in Kyushu to take his physical exam.

About six months later, near the end of the year, I had a postcard from Toyota. "The day I enter the army is fast approaching," he wrote. "Perhaps I shouldn't just come out with it and say so, but it's been a while since I last saw you. This is the send-off party I want.

Everyone contributes ten yen. Where we hold the party itself doesn't matter, but I'd like us to gather first at that coffee shop where you and I used to meet. The Loonies bunch will be there, too. I really want to see you."

On the day, nostalgic affection for Toyota and gratitude for his generosity encouraged me to set off gladly, full of eager anticipation. Maybe I was wholly without shame, or maybe I was just babyishly naïve. Once I'd sent Toyota off to his induction exam, it was as though I'd glimpsed my own dark shadow; I turned away from him as well as from the rest of the bunch, and I avoided places where I might run into them.

On the second floor of the coffee shop where we'd agreed to meet, I found only W. This gave me a bad feeling. It was still early, of course, and W was such a proper fellow that his being the first to arrive meant nothing in particular, but for some reason I'd never much liked him. However, Toyota soon showed up.

W and I had on student uniforms, while Toyota wore an Inverness cape over Japanese dress. From the fold of his robe he took out a pack of Shikishima cigarettes—not a brand you often saw on sale—and casually lit one.

"What about M and Y?" I asked.

"I'm sure they'll be here soon."

It isn't that I'd seen nothing at all of Toyota over the past six months, because we'd met up at odd intervals. This time, though, I felt as though it had been a good ten years. His postcard hadn't encouraged any great intimacy, but I'd counted on our being able to maintain at least a superficial friendliness. What passed between us, however, was something quite different.

"I wanted to get here earlier," Toyota said, "but my car's taillights went out on the way."

"Taillights? You must mean headlights."

"Really? Yes, I suppose you're right. I've forgotten every last word of English."

Whereupon Toyota remarked that he'd collect our contributions to the party expenses now, since the others were late, and he stuck out his hand to receive them. "I'll just go to the toilet," he said and headed downstairs. His figure retreating toward the stairwell, his square, suitcase-like shoulders slanted as always toward the right under his old cape, drew from me a low cry of astonishment.

From behind he looked just like an old man. He might have been forty, he might have been seventy; his back conveyed only an extreme burden of fatigue. That back view of Toyota was my last of him, because an hour passed, then two, and he never came back.

What happened to Toyota Fukumitsu after that I have no idea. I never saw the Loonies bunch again, either, so I wasn't able to ask whether they'd heard anything. From W and others in Toyota's old neighborhood I gathered that he'd died, either in battle in the South Seas or in an air raid on Tokyo. If he died in battle, then I suppose perhaps I was the one who killed him.

Whenever I think of Toyota, I remember for some reason the story of "The King's Ears"—the one about how a barber stole into a grove of great trees that no one knew about and whispered, "The king's ears are donkey ears." I can't help feeling there must be, here and there, groves that have soaked up just such secrets.

The Sword Dance

One vague memory of my boyhood has to do with a sword dance, in which a man with a cushion strapped to his back, representing a baby, fights an enemy while at the same time wiping away his tears. The baby on his back probably keeps the man from wielding his sword freely against his powerful foe, although he wouldn't dream of abandoning it, either. I suppose that's why he's crying. The dance was as boring as it could possibly be, as far as I was concerned, so why in the world did it linger on that way in a corner of my mind? For one reason or another it sometimes comes back to me and plunges me into gloom.

I must have been four or five at the time, and we lived in Koiwa. Presumably this was when my father belonged to a regiment at Kônodai, or some place like that. His comrades got together at our house to drink, and one of them danced with a headband on, waving his sword. That's my very first memory of seeing a sword dance. I wouldn't be surprised if he was wearing a long kimono undergarment of my mother's over his uniform. His face, his hands—in fact, his whole body—impressed me as being bright red. As I watched him dance, my head became heavy and feverish, just as it did when I was sick. I felt so ill I thought I was going to faint. Somewhat later in my life I saw the sword dance performed a number of times, more professionally, in music halls, festival show stalls, and so on. On those occasions, the boy I'd been in the house in Koiwa would always come back to me—my flabby arms and legs, the sensation of pee dribbling down my crotch and onto the tatami, the torn *shôji* doors that sagged when you grabbed the frame to get up. It was a sad feeling, verging on regret. The stage performances I saw tended more toward comedy. After all, a man with a baby on his back has something inherently, perversely grotesque about him, and this one in the bargain is a great swordsman. No one in the audience ever laughed, though. Not that they seemed particularly moved, either. A serious mood filled the theater as they gravely watched the tragically dancing man-with-baby.

Why it is so painful to think of my father? He was hardly an imposing man. His knees wouldn't meet, despite his thirty years in the army, no matter how hard he tried to stretch his legs, and this apparently earned him a scolding by his regimental commander. Moreover, his head had stuck out in front of his chest, like a baby turtle's, ever since he was a boy. During my early days in middle school I once described to him proudly what great equipment the school had. "Really?" he said. "Then I'll have a look myself." That killed my enthusiasm right there. The feeling was far worse that the simple fear of injured vanity.

The year after the war ended my father returned from Indochina. The house in Setagaya, where we'd lived while he was with us, had burned in the air raids, and he joined us at a country retreat my mother's uncle owned in Kugenuma. He arrived with a huge leather rucksack on his back. "Hi!" he said when we faced each other at the door, then fell into an embarrassed silence. Living with him after his ten years away was more like living with a distant relative—an old relative who'd just stopped off on his way to Tokyo and asked to stay a few days. The passage of time did nothing to diminish this feeling; on the contrary, he came to resemble a guest who refused to leave. It was really strange. There we sat, the three of us, around the table at mealtimes, and it was as though an invisible curtain hung before my mother and me—a curtain my father couldn't get through. After emptying his second bowl of rice my father would cock his head reflectively to one side, lift his bowl and mutter, as though to himself, "Look at all the vegetables I have left," then draw his hand back in apparent embarrassment. I was no longer child enough to put on a show of rebellion, but I wasn't sufficiently crafty, either, to assure him with conscious affection, "Father, it's no problem, really." As a result, a silence unbearable to both sides came to separate us. I had a hard time even figuring out what to call him. Before, of course, I used to call him "Daddy," but by now that sounded far too childish. How nice it would have been if we could have just called each other "Dad" and "Son"! But no, that was out. In the end I decided to settle on "Pop."

My father spent almost the whole day in the garden. Once a meal was over he'd practically flee out there, and, no matter what he was doing, he didn't come back till it was pitch-dark. Not even rain could keep him indoors. The first victim of this habit was my raincoat. He ruined it.

One day, about a month after life with father began, there occurred an incident so startling that I can't even remember what kind of day it was. The three of us were sitting together as usual, having our miserable dinner, when I complained to my mother about some little thing or other. Suddenly, my father threw his chopsticks at me.

"What do you mean by talking that way?"

"But . . ." Even as I began my reply, I realized that this was no longer a man I could casually call "Pop." That made things easier for me. I now had a standard for behaving properly as a son.

What *did* my mother think of my father? The question took on renewed urgency. Surely my father was like a guest in the house because my mother loved me more than she loved him? It seems there's nothing unusual about a mother's love shifting more to her children as she gets older. I was still rather anxious, though. I felt as though I was burdened with two quite different kinds of love. Time after time I awoke to hear my mother and father arguing in the room where they slept, across the hall. His low tones muttered on endlessly, as though clinging to her high-pitched ones, and their voices kept me awake even though I couldn't make out what they were saying. By and by I actually came to detest my mother. I couldn't stand merely being next to her. Having a bad back, I spent most of my time in bed, and it especially got to me when she'd plump herself down next to my pillow and gaze vacantly at my face. At those times I'd feel the full extent of my mother's love directly, with my whole body. My face seemed to burn with her physical warmth. I'd avert my eyes and look out toward the garden. The sight of my father brandishing his hoe would startle me, and I'd feel as though I was cheating on him.

"What is he going to do, though, dear?" my mother would ask me from time to time.

"Umm, well . . ." I had no answer.

Needless to say, the family was strapped for money. I did subcontract translation jobs for fashion magazines and so on, but what I could manage, bedridden in a house like that, didn't bring in much—not enough that we could afford any kind of treatment for me.

Now, despite being a professional soldier, my father had actually graduated from the Department of Veterinary Science at Tokyo Imperial University, and he also knew a good many currently prosperous government officials and private individuals from the time when he was in the South Seas. There had to be a chance that approaching them might turn up some sort of work, or at least some way of coming into money. In that sturdy rucksack of his, my father brought home with him British-made blankets, suit cloth, leather shoes, and whatnot, and on his wrist he wore two watches—things almost unbelievable in the possession of a former POW. Earlier, when he came home during the China Incident, my mother and I had been horribly disappointed to find that his luggage, carried by two soldiers, contained only an enormous quantity of broken pottery. This time was quite different. "Some men filled their luggage with sugar and rice," he explained, opening a tin of Navy Cut cigarettes and lighting one with a Moulmein lighter, "but I thought things like this would be more useful." He's doing much better! my mother and I said to ourselves, spreading out the cloth or trying on the shoes. As though to show off his progress toward practical living, he explained how he'd had the rucksack made to accommodate seven pairs of shoes if you undid all its cords.

My mother and I were like an innkeeper who judges the quality of a guest by his clothing and shoes. And we'd completely misunderstood him. We'd assumed for no good reason that he'd support us, as before, from a monthly salary. It never occurred to us that his working from morning till night in the yard and turning most of the lawn into a vegetable patch was, for him, not just a pastime but actual work.

Time made our error ever clearer. Within four months, everything of value from the rucksack had been sold and turned into food, but my father just kept going out to his garden patch. The three of us went on eating our dreary meals. Without a qualm my father started taking seconds again and again, which turned my mother all the way into the innkeeper who, in dealing with a guest who stays on without paying his bill, mingles excessive courtesy with brusqueness. For my part, I cut down what I ate as much as I could, so as to provide a model of frugality. I couldn't say what my father thought privately of either one of us, but at any rate he ate more and more, despite our intentions, and devoted all his energy to his garden patch, the source of this vast appetite.

What we bystanders just couldn't understand was why my father never visited those influential contacts of his. Surely it would have done him good to visit old colleagues, even if they weren't really that influential; but no, far from calling on anyone, he rarely went out his own gate. When he first came home, he'd taken the train two or three times to Tokyo, an hour or so away, and he'd been to Yokohama, too, but lately he showed no interest in going even to the nearby town.

The less he went out, the stranger he looked. Most of the time he wore either my old beret from my student days, or the conical sedge hat he'd brought back from Indochina, clapped on over the peculiar haircut that he gave himself—neither shaved nor long, and ending at the back in a sort of rabbit tail. Over his shirt—a British-made one of fine gabardine, with a proper collar—he wore an underwear top, and, below, either long johns or baggy trousers tied up at the knee with string. The way he worked, like a peasant, the whole outfit was stained with mud and sweat. By now I could hardly stand it to share a meal with him, and the frugality that allowed me to finish as fast as possible was no mere show. My father had always put soy sauce on everything, even apples and bananas, and when it came to food he generally displayed strange tastes alien to others. Now, though, he'd also mash up his sweet potato on his plate, pour water over it, and drink it. Apparently this was his way of bulking up his food as much as possible. "It feels good to get a gulletful when you swallow," he'd say, gulping down a mouthful so as to swell his throat. When satisfied, he'd draw up a knee, give it a few good whacks, and roll his narrowed eyes till the whites showed. He might as well have concocted table manners expressly designed to disgust the two of us.

Now and again my mother would urge my father to go and see Mr. A or Mr. H in Tokyo. I never felt like chiming in on her side,

because as far as I could see there was no way my father in his present
condition could get a proper job and earn any money whatever. Still,
I'd suddenly put in my two cents' worth for her when she brought up
the subject, and my father, stiff-faced, mumbled sounds of apparent
agreement, meantime shaking his head with a moronic grin as
though refusing to listen. If my mother was talking he'd come out
with some remark—joking or not, you couldn't tell—like, "Ah, age
makes you a child again!" But at a word from me he'd turn away with
a stony look.

"Age? Why you're still only fifty-five, aren't you?"

Silence. My father's sunburned face, with its prominent
cheekbones, paled a little. Mouth clamped tight shut, he sat as still
as a rock. I wondered whether he was angry, but then I noticed his
eyes were darting all around the room as though he were looking
for somewhere to hide. After that, I didn't feel like saying another
word.

It's not exactly that my father had lost all trace of self-confidence.
For example, he was proud of every single thing he'd grown in his
patch. The patch wasn't that big—just a sixth of an acre within the
garden—but it was so beautifully done that it wouldn't have looked
out of place at Versailles. In one corner, a seedbed of Sanjô potatoes
bordered a fan-shaped expanse of barley, beyond which grew squares
and triangles of tomatoes and beans. The whole effect was extremely
decorative, but the yield was unlikely ever to reward all the work my
father had put into it. Our land was almost entirely sand, being so
close to the sea, and no amount of fertilizer could get a worthwhile
yield from it. Neither the cucumbers nor the tomatoes grew properly.
The only exception was the tobacco, which as far as we could tell
grew very nicely. Of course, none of us had ever seen a living tobacco
leaf, but from the South Seas my father had brought back the seeds
of some rare variety in a bamboo tube, and he tried planting them to
see what would happen. They grew like mad and put out leaves so big

that it was hard to associate them with a puny little cigarette. Anyway, this tobacco did better than anything he planted, and, tobacco being in such short supply then, even I watered it from time to time and propped up the leaves to make sure they grew straight.

I knew little enough about tobacco processing, but at least I could manage drying the leaves in the shade and chopping them up fine enough to smoke. Figuring out that much was instinctive, so to speak—it seemed obviously right. Moreover, it led to what I think was the very first relaxed conversation between my father and me. There we were on the veranda on the north side of the house, holding the cords that we'd hung there like bunting to dry the leaves, now of a manageable size.

"How does it taste?"

"Huh? Oh, pretty much like the stuff the Burmese natives smoked, wrapped in corn leaves."

"And that's good? Must be better than smoking old leached-out tea leaves."

And so on. It just kept raining and raining, which is no doubt why the tobacco refused to dry.

We tried drying it somewhere else, but that didn't go well either. All we got was a peculiar mass of dark green, withered leaves that disintegrated at a touch into powder. There was no way to shred it. I put some in a pipe and tried smoking it, but it filled my mouth with a powerful stench of burning, dried kelp. Taken aback, I put the pipe down. My father, however, went on puffing away with a dreamy look on his face. "It's good," he said, and he went on about how that was the genuine tobacco taste, how he'd forgotten it, how tobacco as strong as this was the real thing, and how the government undoubtedly mixed a lot of extraneous stuff in with the tobacco you could normally get. He seemed deeply impressed with his homegrown tobacco.

Apart from this tobacco, my father also managed to grow some absolutely enormous sweet potatoes—just one could weigh several kilos, and to me they looked more ugly than anything else—that got him quite excited. Once a change of address card came from one of those influential people he'd known in the South Seas, with a few words written in the corner to inquire how he was getting on. My mother and I jumped on this chance to urge him to go up to Tokyo.

"You don't have to get him to find you a job," we said, "but do for once go and breathe Tokyo air."

Normally, a worried look would creep into my father's eyes when a card like that came and my mother mentioned who it was from, but this time, to our surprise, he actually agreed to go. He had my mother buy him a new pair of socks, and he went to the barber to have his peculiar hair close-cropped in military fashion. On the day it was a whole song and dance, once he had on the suit he never wore, to get his tie out properly over his collar, and despite endless adjustments there remained some sort of mismatch between his costume, his head, and his feet.

"You look great, great!" we assured him, and off he went with a self-conscious air, like someone just discharged from a hospital, carrying a pocketful of his roll-your-own cigarettes.

He returned the following afternoon. He'd been fine when he left, but when he got back he was sick. "I'm cold, so cold!" he said as he rushed into the house and dove straight into bed, the snot dribbling all the way down to his upper lip, like a child. His trousers were so muddy you wondered where he'd been walking during those two days. His coat collar was filthy—he seemed to have thrown up on it. He'd only say that he began to feel ill while warming himself at the brazier at my cousin's (his nephew's) house. For some reason he had no appetite at all, and whatever he tried to eat would come right back up again.

"You didn't go to Mr. H's house?"

My mother put the question to him, but it was pointless to wait for an answer. My father slept on, too weak to talk, with the blue of his freshly shaven head just peeping out beyond the edge of the quilt. The sight filled me with a new kind of sadness. I couldn't help wondering whether he was going to die. His vomit had brown flecks in it—they might be blood. Being such a great drinker, he could easily be suffering from stomach cancer. What bothered me was that the thought of my father's death gave me a certain feeling of relief. Materially speaking, our house resembled a life raft from a sunken ship, and having one fewer on it would be all to the good. It seemed not to do anything for our mood, either, to have my father with us. The more I thought about it, the more I realized that I must not love him at all. I began to think that my mother's and my plot to have him at all costs visit Tokyo might have to do with our wanting to kill him.

Of course, those feelings didn't weigh on me every moment. Sometimes I suspected my father of faking this illness for some reason. He was the type to just love being nursed despite his perennial good health. When my mother happened once to mention the old man next door, who'd been paralyzed for years, my father actually remarked with genuine envy, "Ah, I wish *I* were that sick!"

Each of the possibilities I'd foreseen turned out to be half right. He really could have died, and he really did gladly cultivate his illness. Having no appetite, he derived all his pleasure from his ultra-pure tobacco. Unfortunately, incredible though it might have seemed, this tobacco was also pure poison. More childish than ever after taking to his bed, he'd heave a sigh that could just well have been a reproach, then suddenly call as though in delirium for each of the Taiwanese houseboys who'd served him at the front: "Tarô! Shôkichi! Kiyoshi!" All this aroused my suspicion, and I'd sometimes remark when he reached for the homegrown tobacco he kept by his pillow, "Don't you think you'd do better to give it up?" Every time he'd fix me with a baleful glare, as though to say, "So, you want to rob me of my last pleasure?" I wasn't sure, of course, but to avoid any misunderstanding

I could only watch in silence while my father almost ostentatiously smoked one of those cigarettes that reeked of burning seaweed and sank again into what seemed, judging from the look on his face, an oppressive dream.

This would have gone on indefinitely if my mother had not managed to buy Coronas, a government cigarette brand, on the black market. Actually, my father refused to the very end to believe that his tobacco was poisonous. It's just that when, without a word, we put the Coronas next to his pillow, he instinctively chose them instead, despite the adulterated quality of their tobacco.

My father's health soon returned to normal when it became clear that his homegrown tobacco had been making him ill. One thing didn't return to normal, though, either for my father or for us. It's not exactly that the tension between us relaxed so much that we felt all cozy together; it's more that we fell into a sort of weary resignation about being stuck with one another. My mother and I gave up once and for all urging my father to go and see Mr. H or anyone else in a position of influence. Till then, my father's absurd fear of people, the city, and society in general had utterly exasperated me, but after what had just happened, I gave up expecting him to be able to do anything at all and, at the same time, felt as though I'd settled into some sort of community of spirit with him. It's also perfectly possible that somewhere in his heart my father attributed his illness to a plot devised by my mother and me to make him find a job. After all, despite the obvious consequences of smoking that tobacco, he still refused to discard the grotesquely large leaves and instead put them out stealthily to dry in the shed. On the other hand, he certainly bore us no malice or enmity. What was past was past, and he took what we'd done as the result less of ill will than of unavoidable error. "Well, the main thing is that he (or I, or you) didn't die of it!" That was the thought we all kept in mind.

Was this situation good, or bad? I couldn't say. All I know is that my father stopped behaving like a visitor in the house.

The family's economic plight became increasingly dire. My father began keeping chickens, but all his work went as thoroughly to waste as it had done with the vegetable patch. To keep the chickens going we had to buy feed, and since we never had that kind of money, our kimonos, trousers, blankets, and lacquerware kept disappearing to provide it. Meanwhile, the proceeds from selling eggs slipped through our fingers and melted away before our eyes. The saddest thing about having those chickens, though, was learning how they lived. In my opinion, there's no creature in the entire world as materialistic as a chicken. That's not because chickens exist to be eaten; cattle and pigs, likewise living meat, are far more spiritual. The truth is that a chicken never has a moment of peace. Bloodshot eyes staring wide, they fight continually, as though possessed. During the month it took to put up their coop they lived under the veranda, contained by chicken wire. Their screeches, and the clunk of their heads bumping into things as they ran around down there, came stabbing upward at us the whole time, driving all three of us crazy. The one they most thoroughly affected was of course my father, whose eyes became indistinguishable from a chicken's. My mother went around the neighborhood trading eggs for rations of cornmeal, saying she needed it to feed the chickens, but actually my father ate most of it. This plentiful source of food made him a greater eater than ever. Even outside regular meal times, there he would be whenever he had a moment, leaning over the electric stove, savoring in that special way of his some cornbread he'd baked himself—holding it in his throat, with his eyes turned up to show the whites.

All those chickens did was stoke my father's vast appetite. We had next-to-no profit from them, but trading eggs for feed made us well known in the neighborhood. This time it was my mother who became reckless. She started talking about buying a vast quantity of monosodium glutamate from the nearby S family, who had helped her in her quest for chicken feed, and going into business selling it. Perhaps her feminine vanity had seduced her into dropping hints to Mr. S, or perhaps Mr. S had simply made the assumption on his own, but at any rate, it turned out that my father was thought to be a brilliant scientist. One day, Mr. S suggested in person to my father that they go in together on a joint venture to manufacture soy sauce.

By this time, Mr. S said, nearly two years after the end of the war, there was no profit any more in simply moving goods around. It was now imperative to shift to manufacturing. He had his eye on miso and soy sauce, but he lacked the technical expertise, which he hoped my father would provide. He himself would supply the capital and necessary materials.

Mr. S, who said he had been a policeman in the overseas territories, clearly accepted a highly exaggerated notion of my father's former standing. My father's only experience in that direction consisted of having failed, as a member of a military research unit, in an attempt to extract monosodium glutamate from horsehair.

My father was in no hurry to reply. Actually, he didn't particularly like Mr. S. It wasn't a matter of trusting him or not; for some reason he just didn't warm to him. He'd remark, for example, that he didn't care for the padded kimono Mr. S wore, or that Mr. S's wife and children were ugly. This time, though, he simply had to try anything to make money. Besides, our family had nothing to lose, regardless of Mr. S's character. My mother and I kept reminding him of these realities till he finally agreed.

Mr. S explained initially that he would set up a furnace and other equipment in our garden, but in the end he began with very simple equipment indeed. He just poured salt, coarse monosodium glutamate, and, to provide the color, caramel sauce into a barrel of water and mixed them together. The utter simplicity of the process apparently disappointed my father. I suspect that secretly, despite his distaste for the enterprise, he found Mr. S's plan itself extremely appealing. "I was almost there, you know, when I was working on horsehair," he'd say, earnestly writing something or other down on graph paper. Mr. S, however, ignored these visionary scribblings. He'd bring people over and describe my house to them as "my factory." "This gentleman is my foreman," he'd say, introducing my father. "He used to work in the Army's Sanitary Supplies Stables." Of course, the real factory remained top secret.

Mr. S's buildup must have actually worked because, strange to tell, the soy sauce sold well, and not only in the immediate neighborhood. Some people even came by train to buy it, bringing empty half-gallon bottles.

"Please be patient a moment," we often had to say. "We'll have a new batch ready in half an hour."

By this time the original barrel was too small, so to make the stuff we filled the tub in the bathroom and dumped the salt and so on into that. Everyone liked the flavor so much that at dinner our unsuspecting customers dipped their sashimi and pickles into the resulting liquid.

For a couple of months we dreamed continually of having people after us in hot pursuit. I have no idea how much money we made. Making and spending all this money turned our heads. On Mr. S's orders my mother had repeatedly to carry large boxes of monosodium glutamate back from Tokyo, keeping an eye out meanwhile for the economic police. We also had to be on the lookout constantly, in case our secret factory was under surveillance. On top of that, a stream of people we didn't know—a dozen or more each day—kept coming to the house. Mr. S seems to have been a relatively nice fellow, for someone engaged in that type of business, but his wife and children turned up almost daily to spend their time hanging around "my factory."

A sort of criminal look crept into my parents' eyes, as though a second, strangely luminous and ever-shifting pupil had developed there. In short, this probably wasn't the life for us. Then one day we did at last something we should never have done.

We'd halted production because our supplier happened to be out of caramel sauce, and we offered to sell soy sauce made only of water, salt, and monosodium glutamate. The customer, probably some household's maid, looked doubtfully at the bottle of colorless, transparent liquid she'd been given.

"The color makes no difference, you know," we assured her. "It's the same thing." Why did we do it? By chance all three of us were there, and not one thought anything of it.

After that the stream customers suddenly stopped. In no time the whole neighborhood knew our soy sauce was fake. For some reason, they'd greet us more politely than ever when we stepped out the gate.

We'd had no real income during our soy sauce dealing days, but what with one thing and another there had always been money on hand. Once the business collapsed, we were even worse off than before. Our situation then had been like that of someone tortured by fantasies. The poor—and also people troubled by debt—generally suffer from vain fears the way people do from a chronic disease. What's to become of me, they keep wondering. Now, though, my family's plight more and more resembled an acute toothache. Having sold practically everything we owned in the way of clothing, furniture, and other daily necessities, we also had to slaughter and sell the chickens in which we'd invested the proceeds in the hope of getting it all back. My father, who was obliged to wring their necks one by one, starting with the poorest layers, would crawl on all fours into the chicken coop and get his hands and cheeks scratched every time by the desperately struggling chicken.

Under the circumstances we had no choice: we had to revive our campaign to make my father look for a job. We'd already given up, though, on getting him to visit Mr. A or Mr. H. It's not so much that there was no point in trying; it's more that, for third parties like my mother and me, such men of power and influence had become fictions consisting of only a name and a photograph. Just once, my father volunteered to go and see the director of the Tokyo Zoo. The fellow gave him ten duck eggs to take home, but the train fare and associated expenses involved in this venture had an unfortunate effect on the entire family budget.

Desperate as we were, a new misfortune now delivered us a decisive blow. We were burgled. We never imagined a burglar finding anything to steal, even if one got in, but one night, while we slept, we were robbed of the entire contents of the three-mat room next to the toilet, the one we used as a closet: one overcoat, two military uniforms, two suits (more or less shared between me and my father), and three kimono, with their obi sashes, belonging to my mother. Now we *really* knew what it means to be stripped bare. In fact, if we didn't manage to replace all this, we'd be as thoroughly skinned as the white rabbit of Inaba, after the sea monster got him. We wouldn't even be human any more. It would take just too much explaining to get people to accept our walking around only in nothing but long johns and shirts. Half the day went by while my head remained empty. Try as I might to dream up some way out, the idea that the clothes I'd been wearing were gone for good made me feel as though I'd vanished myself, and I just couldn't get beyond that. My mother, being a woman, just about went crazy. Only my father behaved as though nothing had happened. He went out with his hoe precisely as usual to work in his vegetable patch, wearing his same old baggy trousers tied up at the knee with string.

The next day I made up my mind and set off for Tokyo, where I actually found my father a job—a rather unusual one, though.

K, a friend from middle school, had worked as a houseboy for an American army officer who'd liked him so much that K had gone on working for him even after graduating from college. There was even talk of the officer taking him back to America. Not having seen K for quite a while, I went to visit him without any particular hope. It turned out that he was currently employed as an interpreter by the Security Department of GHQ.

K listened to my story.

"I see," he said. "I may be able to help you, if a house guard job will do. We're talking about your old man, right?"

"Sure, that's fine. Is it hard work?"

"No, there's really nothing to it. Apparently, about all you have to do is sleep next to the boiler room. It amounts to being a sort of guard dog."

That sounded fine to me. In fact, it was positively thrilling. Lately my father had stopped looking frightened when talk turned to his getting a job. With his blasé smile, he seemed to be affecting outward desperation and inner pain over the conviction that no one could possibly hire him for anything, but actually to be quite happy about it.

I was surprised when I got home to find my parents drinking cheap *shôchû* liquor together. My mother was wearing work pants some neighbors had given her because of the robbery. They must have been too small, because I could see her underwear through the side seam.

"I went to Tokyo today, to help find father a job," I announced.

Silence.

Both of them seemed to be speechless. I told them what K had said.

"Won't you give it a try?" I went on, encouragingly.

My father shone a dim light on his face, turning it dark brownish-red. "Don't talk nonsense!" he said and stood up to go in to bed.

I was furious. "All right," I roared back, "then you can damn well go and look for a job yourself! *I'd* keep looking till I dropped!" From behind the sliding panel there came no reply. My mother hadn't said a word. Because of the day's journey, my first in a long time, as well as the ensuing agitation, my heart felt that night as though it were beating painfully against the diseased part of my backbone.

The next morning, my mother came to me to tell me that my father wanted the job and hoped I would introduce him to K. This news put me in the gloomy sort of mood, painfully compounded of vanity and regret, that I used to experience in middle school when he told me he was going to visit one of my classes.

My father said he could go alone, but I accompanied him to K's place and then to meet M, the house guard supervisor. We each wore a suit borrowed from a neighbor.

He cheered up surprisingly once he was on the job.

This man who had been developing more and more of a permanent stoop at least lost his fear of going out. From where I lay I could hear him slam the door every time he went out the gate. Being on duty every other day, he could go on passing the time with his vegetable patch, and his Versailles-style crop beds took on a remarkably jaunty air. The first time I saw him in the outfit the color of blue paint that he called a US Army uniform, I could hardly believe how much he'd changed. During his thirty years in the Japanese Army he'd never once managed to stand with his knees properly together, but now he seemed to have some sort of talent for looking at home in his uniform, which he also wore to work in his vegetable patch. It obviously meant a lot to him.

"There's really nothing like a monthly salary!" my mother would say, naturally very pleased. On his first payday my father sent my mother out to buy saké and sweets. It was twenty-two months since he'd been demobilized.

You could see at a glance how nervous and irascible M, the supervisor, was, and besides, I worried how my father might be getting on; so I went to see K and ask him some discreet questions. When hanging out at headquarters with the other house guards my father was, I gathered, a different man from the one we knew at home. K said he told some wonderfully racy stories. "He *was* a vet after all," K laughed. "Every one of his stories has an elephant or a tiger in it." He added, "You're exactly like your old man, you know—your gestures, everything." Blushing, I suddenly realized that I'd been behaving like my father's guardian, and that I'd fallen into the delusion that he was my son.

His salary wasn't enough, but month by month we managed somehow, and when at the end of the year he brought home a bonus, I felt as though I'd finally extricated myself from this feeling that I was my father's father. He even got a raise. About the same time, though, he started becoming edgy and irritable. Sometimes he'd leap to his feet with a great shout in the middle of the night, apparently dreaming a burglar had gotten into the house he was guarding. Whenever he was late coming home we'd do our best to dismiss the idea that something might have happened to him, but we feared the worst anyway. At home, too, he wore that uniform of his all day long. He even slept in it. The skin of the bare throat and chest visible under his blue shirt looked terribly old.

One day my father came back looking lost. "I got fired," he said. Apparently a military inspector had found him standing at the kitchen door, drinking coffee a maid had given him.

Could that really have been reason enough to fire him? Did they suspect him of stealing food? It must have to do with his slacking off on the job, but he'd already been working for some time—couldn't they let him just take a moment for a cup of coffee? When M, the supervisor, called him on the carpet, my father apparently didn't defend himself and meekly accepted his dismissal notice.

Quite apart from whether or not this explanation made any

sense, I couldn't help wanting to know more, so I went to M's house in Shimo-Meguro.

I'd disliked M ever since I first laid eyes on him. To me, he looked mean. Avoiding the mud along tortuous little streets, I made my way to his house only to be told he was out. I therefore retraced my steps as far as Meguro Station, killed two hours, and went again. If I didn't get to see him this time, I told myself, I'd have to conclude that he'd actually been there all along.

He was at home. The moment he recognized me by the dim light in his entrance, however, he asked me to leave. "I don't conduct consultations at home," he said rapidly, flapping his hand at me like a fan.

That brought me up short. To be turned away that bluntly felt ridiculous. While I stood there mumbling, M kept repeating, "Please, I'd like you to leave *now*." Then he added, "There's nothing I can do for your father. It's an order from the Security Officer."

In short, I left again without having had a chance to say a single word.

Yes, it was ridiculous. Presumably my father had been done in in the same way. Before long I was quite annoyed, though—not with M, but with myself and also with something less easy to define. M's metallic voice seemed still to be ringing in my ears—all the more clearly, in fact, the further I got from his house.

Suddenly I got an urge to go and see K. The day of his departure for America with Lieutenant Colonel C, his employer, was fast approaching. (If only K had still been working for GHQ, he might have been able to do something about M.)

I phoned C's house in Harajuku. Fortunately, K was there, and he asked me to come over.

K was apparently treated there like a member of the family. I found him on the second floor, packing up his books.

"They all went to Atami today," he said. "Stay the night, if you like. I don't think you've ever tasted my pork chops."

His smile flashed the white teeth in his suntanned face. In the six months since I'd last seen him he'd filled out more generously than ever, to the point where he was practically bursting out of his trousers.

"What are you going to do over there?"

"Play baseball! Otherwise, I have no idea. I'll hire myself out as a farmhand and take my time thinking about it."

He'd undoubtedly do well wherever he went. Being an orphan, he'd had to work his way most of the time even through middle school, but there was never a trace of anything dark about him. While we talked, I felt his brightness of spirit pass over to me. I forgot all about the failed campaign to save my father's life once I'd enjoyed a good dinner and downed a Coke in the white porcelain bathtub. Then I slept in the bed K kindly made for me on the sofa.

The next day, K came with me to Shibuya, and we decided to have lunch together. K said he was hungry for perfectly ordinary Japanese food, and I had no objection. However, his way of choosing the place was so odd that I found it less incomprehensible than downright disappointing. We walked right past the crowded rows of painted eateries till we came almost to the end. "This looks OK," K said. It was a dim, ramshackle place for people with ration tickets. "I just can't eat this sort of stuff any more," K whispered, glancing significantly at the glass case of reddish-brown giant radish, stewed fish, and boiled green soybeans in their hairy pods.

"What'll you have?" he asked, peering into my face, then held up two fingers to order "Tempura, two tempura."

I hastened to decline.

"Tofu for me," I said.

I shouldn't have refused K's kind offer that way, but I really didn't want a case of hives. K misunderstood me, however. He added an order for tofu as well.

I was pretty well exhausted. My head was heavy, and my mouth too warm. Sitting there opposite K, with whom I'd be talking continuously since the day before, was beginning to weigh on me. I could feel my appetite drain away while I sat there listening to the singer on the radio, registering in my head little but the clanging of a bell.

"All right, here it is!" K announced cheerily, presumably to raise my spirits, as he lined up the dishes before me. Unfortunately, his thoughtfulness was more and more of a burden, and I was tempted to feel annoyed.

I must have been looking glum. It's not a good idea to impose too much on people's good will, I said to myself as I picked up my chopsticks. Then, the moment a few rice grains melted in my mouth, I experienced a strange sensation. I choked, the rice turned hot and bitter, and tears sprang to my eyes. I've had it! I thought, but there was nothing I could do to combat this utterly incomprehensible emotion.

The gloomy German song from the radio next to my ear sounded for some reason like the one that went with the sword dance. The "Ja" or "Ich" sung in a monotonous male voice, the breaks between words breathlessly drawn out, pounding with ominously repeated notes on the piano, brought to mind the swordsman with the white band around his head and the child on his back. Like the pee a child finally releases, half in spite and half for the pleasure of surrender, my tears began their uncontrollable flow and dripped down into my rice bowl. I looked up, and my tear-filled eyes seemed to see everything through layers of strange lenses. Myself as a growing baby; my father in his house guard shirt, hoe raised amid clouds of dust; his glittering medals; my mother's thighs bursting out of those work pants—images like these kept alternating with that of a man caught up in a sword fight while shackled hand and foot by that child, till all of them came to look the same. Then I noticed K's powerful figure moving in front of me. From the pocket of his red-and-white checked shirt he took a handkerchief and offered it to me like a kindly policeman.

"Now, now! What's the matter? There you are, crying and crying—why, it just doesn't make sense!"

The Medal

(1)

After the war, I worked for a while as a cleaner in the Daiichi Sôgo Building, where MacArthur had his office.

"Why'd you do a thing like that?" people sometimes ask.

"I was down-and-out," I answer. "My dad was attached to Army General Headquarters in Indochina, and I assumed he'd killed himself." Or, "It was something new. I'd wanted to get in with the Americans and have a good look at them." Or, "It was a great place for cigarette butts." Actually, I myself hardly knew. I have an idea that I chose the job with brave resolve after long, mature thought, but I also have a notion that I just waltzed into it on a whim. I do remember my immediate motive, though. I was desperate for tobacco, even if I had to smoke butts.

On the subject of picking up butts, I have another memory to relate.

I think it was about a month before Japan surrendered that I spent a whole day wandering around Tokyo with a long, one-puff *kiseru* pipe. (Having joined the army when students were mobilized for departure to the front, I'd been discharged and released from the A Branch of K Military Hospital on June 30, 1945.)

My house had burned down, and for lodging I was imposing on my uncle. They asked me to go and buy rice, but instead of heading for the Chiba countryside, as I was supposed to do, I took the opposite direction and ended up roaming the streets of Tokyo.

I knew perfectly well that I wouldn't find any rice there, and in fact the city was completely empty. In the hospital in K City, which had never been bombed, I used to imagine what cruel fantasies bombed-out buildings and roads wrecked by fire might suggest. From Honchô near Nihonbashi and on to Muromachi, Kyôbashi, the Ginza—on and on I went, and there wasn't a soul to be seen. Some areas lay in ruins, others had escaped the flames, but dead silence reigned everywhere. No voice hailed me. The air seemed eerily clean and was not at all hot, even though it was midsummer.

"No one, no one . . ." I muttered senselessly as I walked along, eyes to the ground. Somewhere along the way I'd acquired the habit of looking down.

Back when they allowed me out of the hospital in K City for trips into town, people everywhere bowed to me because of all the wounded soldiers. It was an old, dark castle town in the north, but I nonetheless kept running into girls in the bloom of youth. They'd be wearing flower-patterned field trousers or Dutch peasant trousers, with a handkerchief pinned to the chest. They'd straighten up when I gave them an unconscious stare, look right at me, and bow very politely. It's not that I was now dressed like a wounded soldier. I had on much poorer, thoroughly worn, synthetic fiber trousers that looked ready to melt off me at any moment, and over them gaiters— the very picture of someone in from the country. Nonetheless the terror of all that bowing, back then, had eaten into my heart and still showed no sign of disappearing.

Of course, I wasn't keeping my eyes down just to avoid having someone bow to me. One of the talents I'd acquired from my time in the army was picking up things that had fallen to the ground. Ah, we'd had to pick up so many things—wire, cartridge cases, trouser knee patches . . . When a soldier looks down, he's bound to have to pick up something. In fact, he need only look, and he'll find most of what he requires right there under his gaze. As I strolled along, with a prayer in my heart and hard-pressed by necessity, all of a sudden a rice spatula would turn up in a grass clump, or a sword clasp between laundry flagstones, and be just what I needed.

Here in the city, however, none of the things I'd have expected to come across turned up at all. Not that I especially imagined anyone hawking rice in the streets—it's just that none of the odd finds I'd have expected to make were there to be found. In the way of a find, a butt or two would have done nicely, but I was really looking for something as humble as possible. To tell the truth, in a corner of my mind I felt unbearably guilty about wandering around this way without buying the rice I'd promised my uncle to get. I'll never be able to go back, I said to myself. Meanwhile, all I had in my pocket was some money that promised nothing at all. However, like someone who's just fallen asleep, I was drawn along through the empty city as if by an irresistible force. Perhaps I was in a state of what they call lethargy or stupefaction. I'd forgotten all the harsh constraints that normally restricted my every move. I registered next to nothing beyond the present moment. No doubt that, too, was an attitude nurtured in me by my army experience: in that world, our only pleasure was "forgetting." Nonetheless, I suddenly remembered the route I used to follow alone—a two-hour round trip—to go and clean the commander's residence. The closer I got to the barracks on my return, the gloomier I felt. Compared to *that* journey the present one was pure pleasure, even though I knew it might mean running out of food. I might die of starvation, but at least my time until then was my own.

However indifferent to the thought of death, though, I didn't seem to be insensitive to hunger. As my spirit weakened, desire began to manifest itself in strange forms. Each night I was tormented by dreams of food that vanished when I went to eat it. My uncle, who slept next to me under the same mosquito net, would tweak my ear every time to wake me up.

"Hey! Hey! What are you smacking your lips for that way? You're making so much noise I can't sleep! Stop it!"

In sober truth, however, my uncle ate three times more than I did. I wasn't especially hungry. On the spiritual level, the very act of eating was becoming distasteful to me. Nevertheless, the ghost of appetite seemed to be flitting constantly around me, unnoticed. It undoubtedly caused the emptiness I felt as I walked through the city.

At last I saw it: the ghost of a butt. I've forgotten the name of the neighborhood, or of the big building that must have been nearby. What I do remember is walking vacantly along and coming to a big trash bin in a corner, under a skinny ginkgo tree with dried-up bark. So far, my roaming endless little streets had yielded three useful butts that I'd refrained from smoking along the way in my *kiseru*. Instead, I stuck them in my pocket and dreamed as I wandered on of pausing, once I had about enough for the length of a regular cigarette, to smoke them somewhere nice like Kachidoki Bridge, while enjoying a river breeze that smelled of the sea.

Suddenly I saw, casually abandoned on the concrete at my feet, a length of straw rope. Why? It looked like good rope, with real value. It might easily be the most useful object left lying around that day in the whole sector of the city I'd walked through. That abandoned length of rope struck a pleasant note of waste among such excessively tidy streets. Stuffed into the black trash bin, the overflowing straw shed a golden glow.

"Just look at that!"

Sure enough, four or five cigarettes lay there, caught in the straw—big, thick ones, and yes, only half-smoked. That's what I saw, I swear it.

"Gotcha!" With a cry I dashed unthinkingly closer, whereupon those cigarettes just blew away on the wind. I picked them up as they rolled toward me. They were only paper tubes. I was neither discouraged nor embarrassed. I wasn't even amused at having been fooled by some bits of straw. That's how down-and-out I was.

(2)

The war ended. That meant I was out of a job for good. Until that very day, and for as long as I could remember, the war had so thoroughly governed my every emotion that I just couldn't manage to believe the Emperor's broadcast. His curiously modulated delivery was so bizarre that all I got was the anxious feeling something extraordinary was going on. Reality notwithstanding, I became convinced after His Majesty's broadcast that the world would soon be plunged even deeper into war, and so the next day I sought refuge at Mount Minobu, where my mother had been evacuated. The place offered no food at all, but there was no need to worry that the enemy might turn up. The head temple of the Nichiren sect of Buddhism was there on the mountain, but you never heard a sound from those round, flat Nichiren drums. Like me, the people there were simply unable to grasp the idea that the war was over. They feared that banging on drums might reveal their location and invite an air raid, and that the enemy might want to come and bomb this mountain because it was the very center of Japanese religion.

It's American cigarettes that really convinced me the war was over. After two months on Mount Minobu I went to see how things were going in Tokyo, and there my friend K gave me a pack of Lucky Strikes.

"OK, I'm going to listen to a French broadcast now," he said and turned to an enormous radio he'd put together.

I couldn't figure out how to open the pack, never before in my life having encountered this brand. Still, the effect, when I tried smoking one, was to bring back something forgotten. The cool, sweet air entering my mouth gave new life to that something, just as meeting someone you haven't seen since childhood revives old memories. Everything around me looked crystal clear, as though a darkened lamp suddenly began to blaze with light. The way people went around with a thin floor cushion around their neck, for example, the way some stuck their noses right into a can to eat from it, or the spectacle I myself made, picking up cigarette butts—everything like that stood out sharply in an entirely new light.

It was a kind of dream. Since reality ends up being dreamlike, this dream was one of being awake. Still, it kept coming back to me. No doubt it signaled the beginning of my spiritual recovery. Certainly those desires of mine, the ones that kept fluttering around me like ghosts, were assuming ever-clearer form. I wasn't as far along yet as my friend K, who'd built a radio to listen to French broadcasts, but at least I now had the gumption to want *something*. The way my hair was growing out (I'd never thought about it on Mount Minobu, where all I saw was shaven-headed priests, but the craze for growing long hair was spreading like wildfire) or successfully trying on the suit of my father's that I'd fished up from the bottom of a trunk—things like that, although nothing in themselves, gave me hope and the pleasure of feeling I'd found something to hold onto.

From the outside, this tendency of mine no doubt made me look utterly idiotic and somewhat crazy. Anyway, the nostalgia aroused by my youthful fantasies moved me to choose carefully among my limited wardrobe, with the result that my extraordinary clothes attracted many a stare. Over a black suit from the early 1920s I'd wear a half-cape made from a Cheviot check lap robe of my grandmother's, with on my head a beret consisting of a student cap with the badge and visor removed. I knew better than anyone else how odd I looked. That's why I dressed that way. I was secretly determined to have everyone else accept my outfit.

A smile would spread across my face as I contemplated myself in the mirror, and I'd whisper, "Aha, they're really going to hate me!"

Nonetheless, in another sense I was proud of my getup. It was weird, yes, it was in bad taste, but such judgments were at best relics of the past. The artless splendor of the Cheviot check pattern, the simple elegance of a dark suit from the Taishô era—wasn't the total effect, in silhouette or in coloring, so extraordinarily powerful as to be overwhelming? So at least I said to myself. Far from regarding my attire somewhat cynically, I felt sure it looked really good—at least, until a trifling incident came along to change my mind.

It happened early one evening at S Station, where two suburban rail lines meet. The friend I'd gone to see had turned out to be away, besides which I was already in a bad enough mood anyway when I started home. The platform was packed because the train just wasn't coming; the wind was cold; the station's feeble lighting was very dim once the sun went down; and the passengers just kept crowding in. To pass the time I took from my pocket a cigarette I hadn't quite finished smoking and put it in my *kiseru*, but I had no matches. So there I was, the *kiseru* in my mouth, looking around for someone else smoking. There was a tug at my sleeve.

"Hey, Daddy-o, try one of these."

A Korean-looking boy in his mid-teens was holding out an open pack of American cigarettes. Not understanding what was going on, I nodded but lost my cool at the same time.

"No thanks, no thanks."

I waved a vigorous refusal. I just didn't have the leeway to buy stuff like that. But the boy kept waving the pack in front of my nose.

"It's OK, it's OK," he said. "Take one!" He meant he just wanted to give it to me.

Now I was all confused, both because I couldn't make out his motive and because I didn't know how to decline his offer. I could have cited plenty of reasons for turning it down, but it was hard to choose an excuse among so many. My dithering suddenly revealed to me I'd turned into a nationalist, and I saw myself as utterly vile. Wasn't I taking this attitude toward him because I assumed he was a Korean? Actually, each of the cigarettes peeping out of that glittering package called to me with a whiteness from which I preferred to avert my eyes.

"Your saying no proves you despise him for no reason," my conscience began whispering to me; to which I replied aloud, "All right, just one."

"Go right ahead," the boy said with a satisfied smile. He gave me a light and stuck two more cigarettes in my pocket, then with the same hand tugged at my Cheviot cape. "That's *nice!*"

Aha, so you gave me cigarettes because you liked my cape, did you? But the cape mattered much less to me than the cool, sweet smoke flooding my mouth. After all, I'd walked the streets picking up butts. Never mind if my outfit no longer brought a frown to the faces of those who fancied themselves men of the world, or punctured their pretentiousness. Could there be anything wrong with my feeling a certain kinship of spirit with this Korean youth?

"Ha, ha, ha!"

"Ha, ha, ha!"

We both laughed. Just then a train arrived on the opposite platform. The youth apparently meant to board it, since he hastily picked up the kerchief-wrapped bundle that he'd put down on the platform's stone paving. Then he turned back toward me, tapped me on the shoulder, and uttered words so terrible that I blanched.

"Well, it's our world now. Let's make the best of it, you and I."

Fully believing that I was his countryman, he dove through the train's automatic doors.

(3)

It occurred to me that I'd better find myself a job before winter came.

Ever since that incident with the Korean I'd lost all ambition, all fastidiousness in matters of dress as of everything else, and as far as a job was concerned, I had no particular wishes. Newspaper reporter, Occupation Army mail censor, teacher, hotel interpreter—most of my friends had jobs like that, but I couldn't see myself as suited to any of them.

I heard of a job that paid 150 yen for just two hours of work a night. The tip came from an acquaintance in his mid-fifties. Being married to a hairdresser, he had no need to work himself. He gave me his name card, and off I went with it to the Daiichi Sôgo Building, which had been requisitioned by the US military. Apparently it was the Maintenance Section that was hiring. Maintenance? Having airplanes on my mind, I imagined in the depths of the building a huge, intricate engine that I would spend the small hours of the night polishing, but no. I was to be a cleaner. If an engine had really been involved, I'd have probably fled then and there. The mere sight of several dozen WACs typing away in broad-shouldered rows made me feel as though hundreds of tiny hammers were whacking away at *me*. If all I had to do was collect the trash from the floors and stairs, however, I was happy to put myself up for the job. It was just made for me, I knew it.

Sure enough, the Maintenance Section suited me perfectly. Being a sweeper basically meant less cleaning the offices and hallways than incorporating all manner of rubbish into one's own person. By the time I'd been at it for a week, that suit I mentioned, and the beret, and the shirt were redolent of rotten, moldy fruit. Item by item the trash was dry and light, but all those bits together gave off a damp, oppressive smell. And what a lot of them there were to collect!

Outside the building you could walk a mile and still find only a few butts, but inside they were just one kind of utterly commonplace garbage. Strange to say, starting work as a "sweeper" (the simple name the Americans applied to all Maintenance Section personnel) suddenly got me going and filled me with life. Wielding American-made brooms and cleaning rags, jumping into the trash bins to tread down the contents so as to make room for more, wheeling the bins onto the elevator and taking them down to the boiler room in the sub-basement—in tasks like these I found for the first time ever all the pleasures of sport. It was as though trash were the very source of my energy. As its smell came to permeate my whole body, every notion of mine about inferiority or degradation seemed to go utterly numb. The American soldiers began calling me Mickey or Joe, and I answered them with alacrity.

"Hey, Joe!" one would call out and hand me half a cigarette he'd had enough of smoking. Needless to say, I'd plunk it straight into my mouth, oblivious of the bad breath that still clung to it. I'd pick up dropped butts, too; but it would have been crazy of me to refuse one actually handed to me, and just double trouble to put it out when it was already burning, only to light it again later on. The soldiers on night duty, seated alone before a telephone that might ring at any moment, were especially eager to talk to us, and we carefully took our time mopping around them, because sometimes they'd give us brand-new cigarettes. Now and again I myself would look for an opening and strike up a conversation. My English was poor, and on top of that the soldier would have an accent that made our words fairly incoherent.

One soldier kept a violin on the desk in front of him.

"You like music?"

"I like it," I answered.

"What's your instrument?"

"Double bass." That was the only instrument I could remember the name of.

He leaned forward over the desk. "Jazz or classical?"

"Classical."

"Yeah? Really? How many in your orchestra?"

"I play solo." I kept my reply simple because I couldn't really understand him.

He was amazed. "You play music for solo double bass?" he asked.

"There's just one piece."

At this point, I'd quit and push my mop off elsewhere unless he gave me a cigarette. If I felt I was getting somewhere, I might add, for example, "It's by a Japanese composer." I wasn't lying or anything. It's just that I wanted a smoke. That's what made me do it. The same compulsion seemed to be driving a lot of other people as well. In trains, for example, I'd seen people crawling around on all fours, frantically hunting for a bit of burning tobacco they'd knocked out of their pipe, so as not to miss their next puff. I thoroughly sympathized. "Ah," I'd say to myself, "he, too, is crawling around on the ground in the hope of continuing his dream."

One evening I came to a halt before Corporal Mitchell. Short and dark-haired, Mitchell was constantly writing letters, which any other soldier would have done on a typewriter. He alone wrote with a pen, always the same one. That was my chance.

The thing is, a medal of my father's had suddenly popped out of the luggage we'd evacuated from Tokyo. It held memories for me. My father had somehow mislaid it, and I, a middle-school student at the time, had been told to go to the divisional officer's club to buy another for fifteen yen. At first I planned to sell this one to the musically minded soldier, but then I changed my mind and turned to Mitchell instead.

That evening, as usual, Mitchell was covering sheets of letter paper with fine, neat writing from his green, slant-held pen.

I asked him whether he was writing to his mother, and he looked up with a smile in his dark eyes and shook his head.

Got him! I'd been right. It was either his wife or his girlfriend. Without a word, I opened the medal's case and put it down in front of him. He gave an awkward laugh.

"You want it? It's for sale."

The medal on its gilt stand was of white cloisonné enamel with, at the center, a glittering red stone.

"How much?"

"In money, 500 yen."

"And in tobacco?"

"I'm not after cigarettes. I'll take your pipe and the tobacco that goes with it. It's a briar pipe, right?"

"Right, it's a 'Morocco' briar. But I've got only two packs of tobacco."

I'd already calculated the price: five packs of tobacco. At this rate, though, I might be able to get double that.

"Two packs—that's not enough."

I was about to reach out and take the medal back when, as though to brush my hand aside, he clamped his hairy fingers onto the medal's black lacquer case.

"I'll bring five more packs on this day next week. OK?"

It was OK. I agreed. In my opinion the pipe, with its pretentious "The Morocco" brand name, actually looked pretty cheap, but the name was seductive anyway, and I suddenly wanted it.

Once I had my hands on "The Morocco," it instantly became my treasured possession. No other accessory ever suited me so perfectly. Once in my mouth, it felt in no time like a part of me. After a day or two, I practically gave up smoking cigarette butt tobacco—not that I didn't feel bad at times about abandoning my old friend.

A strange situation developed, although it didn't last that long.

For some reason or other, the PX ran out of every last cigarette right after Mitchell paid me my five packs of pipe tobacco. The alert sweepers noticed this immediately, because there was no longer a half-smoked cigarette to be found in a single one of their trusty ashtrays, not even in the generals' conference room. (This was no doubt the time when, on the outside, the MPs started cracking down on the possession of American goods by Japanese.) The loser in all this was Corporal Mitchell. At first, every time he ran into me he'd ask me with a complacent smile how I liked his pipe. "It's nice and light, isn't it?" he'd say. In reply I'd mention my medal's glitter and assure him his girlfriend would be amazed. By and by, the sight of me would start him sighing, "Ah, that pipe . . . I really liked it."

Cigarettes were apparently sold out, and we sometimes saw soldiers helping their buddies out with a smoke. Then I came across Mitchell walking at top speed, red-faced, along a corridor miles from his office. In those days I could go into his office, wet mop in hand, stand ostentatiously right there in front of him, and puff billows of smoke from my pipe, and he still wouldn't look in the least amused. Ironically, there still seemed to be plenty of pipe tobacco around. Once a mean-minded soldier showed up in front of Mitchell, held out a box of tobacco, and said, "Mitchell, what's this, written here? I can't read." The soldier refused to leave, and Mitchell had no choice but to read with a sigh the brand name and the jingle-like slogan, "Sweet and mild." Then his cheek sank dejectedly onto his hand, while his elbow rested on the very desk where, in a drawer, that medal was giving off its senseless sparkle.

A Room in Tsukiji

In the spring of my twenty-first year, we all moved to the downtown heart of Tokyo. Why? Because that was the year Komai Kumakichi, who'd dropped out of a Kyoto high school, came up to Tokyo and vaunted to us the art theories of old Edo.

We were convinced at the time that the only thing in life you could believe in was art. For us, it was senseless to become anything but an artist, and to do that you had to lead an artistic life—not that we had the slightest idea what art was, or what an artist was like. Komai's reason for quitting was pretty shocking. He'd grown his hair long, in defiance of the school's rules, but he claimed it was so as to be able to tie his hair into the kind of *chon-mage* topknot men wore in centuries past. According to Komai, "Life in this age so devoid of style has lost all beauty, and whoever wishes to live beautifully must begin by adopting the manners current in the days of the Tokugawa shoguns." Young though we were at the time, we still found his views a bid odd, but his zeal commanded our respect and sharply delineated our still-vague notion of the beautiful. While stopping short of sporting a topknot, we came to entertain the idea of moving to downtown Tokyo, where the customs and manners of old Edo still lived on. The night we decided to do it, we became very excited. The plan was to begin by living together in the same house, where we'd improve each other. Komai, however, opposed the idea, so in the end each of us lived separately, as artists enamored of solitude, in a band along the Sumida River.

Komai found himself a plot at Yanagibashi, Takagi Takeshi a place at Kappabashi, and Yamada Hiroo a spot at Karasumori in Shinbashi, while I took up residence in the Odawara-chô area of Tsukiji. Awkward circumstances prevented only Gotô Morio from slipping out of his parents' house in Aoyama Kitamachi. As a result, he ended up visiting each of us in turn as a sort of day apprentice.

I had one room on the second floor of a cubical house consisting of two rooms upstairs and two rooms downstairs, the house itself being half of a newly built duplex located down the twists and turns of countless narrow streets leading away from the vicinity of the Navy Accounting School. It was a six-mat room, and the rent was twenty yen a month. Later on I realized this was about double the normal market price, but at the time I was only too happy that the landlord was willing to rent it to me at all, and I pounced on it. Komai and Takagi were accustomed to hunting for somewhere to live, being from the provinces, but Yamada and I both had families living in Tokyo, and we felt uncomfortable looking for a place to rent without even presenting an introduction. We knew barbershops and news agents helped students find lodgings, so we hunted hither and yon together, but everywhere we went, the landlord was very suspicious of two youths still in student uniform. We'd had a hard enough time already, just convincing our parents to let us do it. As it happened, my mother had to go and join my father where his office had sent him, and she readily allowed me to go and live elsewhere. She couldn't begin to imagine, though, why we wanted to head for so grubby an area. Anyway, we managed somehow to talk our parents around, but every prospective landlord seemed to take us for ne'er-do-wells.

"You see, it's just that we'd like to experience the atmosphere of old Edo."

The more we came out with things like that, standing there in the entrance to some prospective landlord's house, the stranger the looks we got. They probably imagined we were student delinquents involved in some sort of illegal conspiracy. Inevitably, they answered that although the room *had* been available until just recently, a relative would now be coming to live in it. Under these circumstances, my joy obliterated every other consideration when the owner at Odawara-chô accepted me without a word. This quiet, long-faced man in his mid-thirties was a prawn broker at the Tsukiji fish market. His wife, in her mid-twenties, seemed very nice.

"We apologize for taking so much rent," she said when I paid her the advance, "but, you see, the house was built after the start of the war in China—that's why it's so high." Her manner prompted me to inquire frankly about something that concerned me far more than the rent.

"Could yours possibly be an old Edo family?" I asked.

She smiled brightly. "My husband's ancestors were retainers of the shogun," she replied. I was satisfied. Actually, the second-floor room she took me to wasn't quite all I'd had in mind. The cream-colored walls, the plywood ceiling, the frosted glass panels of a window giving onto the street—none of this conveyed a trace of the mood of old Edo; quite apart from which, I was startled to see hanging, on the wall in one corner, a printed reproduction of calligraphy by General Tôgô.

The calligraphy read, "On this battle hangs the fate of the nation." Perhaps that's what filled me with a vague foreboding.

I got my luggage up there and spent my first night in the house. I'd never before lived in a place I'd chosen myself, and that alone filled me with emotion. The more anxiety and loneliness assailed me, the more I was swept by waves of hope, anticipation, and ambition. Almost as soon as I slipped into bed and turned out the light, though, a pain like an electric shock to the back of my neck concentrated my every thought on that spot. Not for a moment could I believe it was a mere insect bite—it hurt too much. But before I had time to wonder longer what on earth was going on, a second stab came in another spot, and then a third. It felt as though stag beetles were attacking me from all sides. I turned on the light, and there they were: small, black, bean-sized bugs fleeing straight for the nearest wall. I turned off the light and tried to sleep, but they got me again. This was no surprise, though. The way they took turns biting me, they kept me sleepless all night, but the experience was less painful than stirring. I hadn't imagined it happening quite like this, of course, but they certainly brought it home to me that I'd stepped into a world I'd never known before. In fact, the swollen, smarting places around my neck reminded me somehow of the stickers on a traveler's suitcase.

That's how I spent my first night soaking up the "atmosphere of old Edo."

We all lived separately, but we met somewhere every day. We told each other all about the aesthetic lives we were leading.

Any observer would have agreed that Komai Kumakichi's was the most successful of all. After quitting school he'd shaved his head and taken up wearing an old-fashioned outfit bought from a used clothing dealer, with a stiff sash. Even his way of walking, with his back slightly bent, had an idiosyncratic touch to it, giving his gait a character all its own. Whenever we met he'd describe his life with zest, carrying on about how his apartment building at Yanagibashi was full of kept women, ever so pretty and kind; about how he refused to eat any rice tainted by foreign origins because it was impure; about how his meal was specially prepared at a fine old noodle restaurant in the neighborhood; or about how all the restaurant's patrons were as versed as himself, or even more so, in the ways of Edo—for which reason he looked forward to taking us there, once we looked the part a bit more. I, however, had nothing at all to boast about this way. The big difference between Odawara-chô in Tsukiji and the place where I'd lived before was that in Odawara-chô the breeze stank all day of fish. The racket started up there very early in the morning. I could only get up and wander across one main street for a look at the fish market, where I'd watch a man cutting a tuna's head into round slices with a cleaver the size and shape of a Japanese sword, or contemplate a harbor police boat towing a drowned corpse along the canal on rope. Not one of these sights had anything to do with the imagined atmosphere of Edo. Most disappointing of all was that my landlord, who should have been a pure child of Edo, had nothing about him to suggest any such thing. When I heard he was a prawn broker at the fish market, I'd pictured a dashing fellow in indigo blue work pants; but no, this descendant of shogunal retainers was strangely drab and surly in color, even to his face, like a dead fish, and he scuffed off to work in rubber boots. Once I bought him some saké, to thank him for having rented me the room, but he was no better able than I to drink more than a little of it.

"I gather that you and your ancestors have been Edo natives for generations," I remarked, hoping at least for some stories about the old Tokyo.

"I suppose so . . . but you could say the same of yours, couldn't you?"

I asked him whether there wasn't something odd about the way I talked, but he said no. The whole thing just became more and more tedious. This quiet couple never said a word about anything I did; except that I'd sometimes turn General Tôgô's calligraphy, which bothered me, around to face the wall or take it down, only to find on my return from elsewhere that it had been put back again. I couldn't begin to understand why they should be so keen on that scroll, but apart from that, I gave up all interest in them.

The way things were, I just couldn't feel at home there, and I spent my time on long walks. When we all got together we'd talk with scorn of the Ginza as the most boring street in Japan's boringest city, but for some reason that's where my steps took me whenever I was alone. Sandals on my feet, munching an apple, I'd purposely wander back streets splashed with red and green electric light. There would then well up from within me an inexpressible dejection, as though I were secretly betraying all my friends, and in my effort to resist it I'd walk on till I almost dropped. Late at night I'd go home exhausted and crawl into the bedding I'd just left spread out there all day, and the bedbugs would be after me again. After all their nightly torments, though, I'd begun to take a liking to them. I learned their ways so well that I could catch any number of them with the greatest of ease, if I felt like it, but they didn't actually bite me that much, and even if they did, I hardly felt it. When now and again I felt bored enough to catch one and crush it under my nail, the resulting burst of foul odor inspired a sort of tender feeling. The whole thing was stupid, and familiarity with these bugs was all I'd gained from my elaborate move. Still, my new knowledge gave me a degree of pride.

Yamada, who moved to Karasumori somewhat after me, met me the next morning. His exceptionally long neck was bright red and swollen.

"It's a disaster!" he began in great agitation. The house where I got a room is a nest of bedbugs. Every house in the area is the same way—apparently, the liquor store is the only one without them in the whole neighborhood. How about *your* place?"

His expression practically begged me to tell him I had plenty of them. It was all I could do not to laugh.

"There don't seem to be any," I replied. "I've never seen one." To make him feel better, I stopped at a drug store we happened to pass and bought him some bandages and itch reliever.

Two months had passed before I knew it. I began feeling a sort of indescribable oppression. Why in the world was I doing this? I felt like leaping to my feet the moment this thought crossed my mind. I wasn't going to school, I wasn't reading books, I was spending my days doing nothing at all. I couldn't imagine, though, that that was the source of my suffering. If pressed, I'd say I might have been having a hard time because I just couldn't manage to have any fun.

Little by little I grew sick of my friends. Just being next to Komai, for example, made me feel like a loser. The things he enjoyed doing didn't appeal to me at all. One evening he turned up at my room and announced that he'd just left the standing-only gallery at the Kabuki-za. The landlord's wife brought tea.

"She's nice, isn't she?" he remarked as her steps faded away down the stairs.

"Nice? In what way?"

"In what way? Well, she's a true Edo beauty, isn't she? In terms of actors, she's a veritable Tokizô."

He had me there. What about her could possibly be associated with any particular good looks? Obviously Komai perceived a kind of beauty to which I was blind. In such a connoisseur's presence, I felt obliged to praise a dish I disliked.

"I suppose so, now you mention it," I managed painfully to respond; whereupon Komai waxed enthusiastic. "Ah, I'd like a stolen moment with her!" he declared loudly. "I'm in love with her!" This was crazy, but I didn't want to hurt his feelings. "Right," I said, spouting utter nonsense, "I get the feeling she sort of likes you, too." The next morning I was startled to note a sour look on the lady's face. She must have overheard everything we'd said the evening before.

"What *is* it with this friend of yours?"

I couldn't even look up at her. However, her concern was entirely practical.

"He went off by mistake with my husband's *geta*."

Sure enough, Komai's grubby *geta* were still there in a corner of the entrance.

That's the way it went every time. Takagi Takeshi caused me grief in another way. The fellow was a poet, but having (as he put it) no faith in words, he wrote exclusively onomatopoeic poetry. None of us knew where he came from or how he'd managed to insinuate himself into our circle, but apparently his poem "*nurupin nurupin nurupin / nurupin nurupin nurupin*" had deeply impressed Komai, and everyone else had admired it, too. Although just a year older than the rest of us, Takagi was thoroughly poised and had everyone's respect. Anyway, at some point he just moved into my room. He hardly ever said a word, and he never laughed. If I said something to *him*, he'd remain silent and answer with a fart. I think he addressed me first only once, suddenly, in the middle of the night.

"Aha!" he bellowed. "Japan has some good poems, too! 'The ocean in spring: / gently rising, sinking swells / sinking and rising.' What do you say to that?"

That was the only time. I was just falling asleep, and I wondered for a moment whether he'd taken leave of his senses. He would spend all day with me. When I went out, he'd accompany me in silence. When he was hungry, he'd stop without a word in front of an eatery. It was no use trying to walk on by. He'd just follow me and stop again in front of the next eatery.

What with one thing and another, I soon ran out of money. The first month, the money my family sent me lasted two weeks, but the next month it lasted only one. The month after that, I redeemed the most necessary items that I'd pawned, and, with the interest payment, what money I had left didn't last me three days. I sold all the books I could and pawned even the phonograph and records I'd borrowed from a friend, but it still wasn't enough. Where was it all going? As far as I knew, I was living far more frugally that I'd done at home, but everything just seemed to cost so much more. I thought perhaps it was because I had Takagi with me, but no. Even when he and I dined out together, we always ate as cheaply as possible. Still, I couldn't help feeling that his simply being with me made the expenses mount up.

I lost every notion of what I was trying to do. Walking around town looking at girls, I forgot what kind of girl struck me as pretty. Even when writing my mother letters riddled with lies, to cadge money from her, I felt as though I were only writing the plain truth. Sometimes I felt like giving the recumbent Takagi, his backside toward me complete with a hole in his trousers, a good, swift kick; but unfortunately, I had no wish to break it off with the whole group.

"Ah, I'd so like to go to school."

So I might whisper unconsciously to myself, then think again and decide I was just being sentimental because I'd pawned my school cap and uniform. I knew what I didn't like in food, but what I did like I had no idea. One rainy day Takagi, by some miracle—heaven knows where he found the money—bought us steaming bean jam–filled pancakes from an eatery at the fish market, and I *did* find I liked mine.

What I objected to was that the question, "What's it all for?" kept nagging me whenever I hung around doing nothing.

Perhaps these same feelings were beginning to oppress us all, because we played rough, unkind tricks on one another. All of a sudden, for no reason, Komai and I backed Yamada up against the railing of Kachidoki Bridge and threw his student cap off into the water. Yamada retaliated by snatching off my hunting cap and doing the same. We watched the two caps bobbing on down the Sumida River toward the sea. This sort of thing went on in broad daylight, while we were still cold sober.

Komai and Yamada had come to my room that day. During a pause in the conversation, Yamada noticed a letter in a woman's writing lying on a bookshelf.

"What's this?" he said. "Why, look, the envelope's still sealed!"

"It's Gotô's," I explained. "Gotô's girlfriend sent it to him, add-ressed to me."

Yamada refused to believe me.

Early that year, Gotô had become intimate with the head maid at a hot spring inn in Fukushima Prefecture. The affair was so serious that he'd flunked out of school, and his parents had naturally forbidden him all further contact with her. (This was also why they wouldn't let him live away from home.) So he got all the mail from his girl through me.

"Have you ever looked inside it?" Komai asked.

"Nope."

"It's incredibly thick. I'd really like a peek inside."

"Yeah, right," I answered vaguely.

I hesitated, although at the time I myself had no idea why.

Just then Yamada put his oar in. "If you want to open the envelope, just peel off the glue," he said. "He'll never notice a thing."

That did it. I tore the envelope open. What emerged from it, however, wasn't at all what we'd expected. No doubt it was perfect under the circumstances: a ten-yen bill wrapped in sheet after sheet of blank letter paper.

"Amazing!"

On the spot we took the money, and off we went. Takagi, who'd listened in silence to the whole conversation about whether or not to open the envelope, came with us. A café in Asakusa, a stage review, a Yanagibashi chicken restaurant that Komai knew well. Determined to make the most of every last penny, we spent the rest on saké, *tsukudani* appetizers, and pickles, then headed for Komai's apartment.

We had a ball that evening. We were all hallucinating. Stealing ten yen convinced us we were now gangsters. But in fact the envelope's having contained paper money probably saved us from actually becoming real ones.

Anyway, we imaginary gangsters then began to plot a genuine

crime. We set about squeezing more money out of Gotô's girlfriend by using him as a decoy. It was Komai who cooked up almost the whole plan. He began by writing her the following letter.

"We are Gotô Morio's close friends, and therefore we are constantly concerned about him. Recently he has been in desperate need of money. He has borrowed large sums from his friends, and, unbeknownst to his strict parents, he has been carrying off their household possessions and pawning them. For a long time we could not imagine why he is so greedy for money, but recently we understood at last that it is because of you. You are older than he. Therefore it is you who seduced him, and it is for that reason that suffering leads him to spend so much. We urge you to send him money. It is your responsibility to do so. If you do not, we will tell everything not only to his parents, in order to put a stop to this affair, but also to your employer. Under such circumstances, it is quite possible that you will be arrested by the police for the crime of incitement."

"It works better at first not to mention any particular sum," Komai declared like a seasoned criminal, adding other ingenious touches and spurring us on to hope that we'd soon be luring her to us and suborning her to our common desire.

"The letter has be in formal epistolary style," Komai announced at last. "All right, you, get busy and write it!" He pointed at me.

"Me? Sure!"

I spent the whole night laboring to give the letter a correct, high-toned formality. At last, the job was done.

While writing the letter I thought nothing about it. The instant I slipped it into the mailbox, however, I suddenly found myself in the grip of terror. I was Gotô's oldest friend. And yet, I felt as though that friendship had been an utter lie. I came to realize that the rest of us had been treating him as a sort of apprentice to the group. What I'd done, and especially my ready willingness to rewrite the letter, weighed on me heavily. Perhaps writing too many lying letters to my mother had given me the ability to write that way. I also quaked with another more down-to-earth, hence still more fantastic fear. Now that I've written that letter, I said to myself, the proof is out there. I'll be arrested for extortion, I just know it!

While these torments swept over me by turns, I waited impatiently for the reply. "She'll probably wire money as soon as she gets the letter," they all said at first. Naturally, nothing of the kind turned up. Nothing either the next day, or the next. My anxiety only grew as the days went by. My imagination took flight, and I pictured in exquisite detail how she might take the letter and how it might then make the rounds to her employer and to the police.

A whole week of waiting later, the answer finally arrived. It was stunningly plain, compared to the agonies I'd been through: "Your letter is so hard I can't understand it. Please make it easier."

"Singing to the deaf": no doubt this was the very meaning of the expression. I no longer knew whether to be relieved or disappointed. Staring blankly at this note from a hot-spring maid, I experienced an indescribable wave at once of sadness and of mirth.

Our plunge into the atmosphere of Edo had turned out very differently from what our initial enthusiasm had led us to imagine. The downtown heart of old Tokyo, where we'd come to add "beauty" to our lives, had welcomed us only with bedbugs and the stink of fish, and in the same way I myself, who believed I'd fallen to the level of a gangster, had failed to achieve even that. The idea that "beauty" resided somewhere, and that we could just go and pick it up, had led us astray. I'd experienced nothing but disillusionment ever since moving to Tsukiji, and by now I lacked the strength of mind to conjure up even the ghost of those ideals. Come to think of it, Komai Kumakichi, who'd first passed that ghost to me, looked pretty dismal too, now that a hot-spring maid from northern Japan had made a fool of him.

Her reply had freed me from the fear of being dragged before the police, which was such a huge relief that it seems to have made me ravenously hungry. That evening Takagi and I had a good wash at a public bath, then stuffed ourselves with soy-flavored omelet and bowls of beef over rice at a neighborhood eatery. To my surprise, we came across a pleasant sight on the way home.

It was nearly the end of June and as hot as any midsummer evening. Bathed in sweat, Takagi and I emptied our bowls, then left the oily stench of the restaurant to stroll along the canal behind Saint Luke's Hospital. Few people took that way after dark. We were leaning idly against the bridge railing when suddenly I saw Takagi mumble something.

"I'll be damned! Look, there's a firefly!"

"Where? Show me! Where is it?"

"Look, look, right over there!"

And there it was: a small, pale, blinking light was flitting about in the inky darkness behind the hospital, among the weeds pushing up through the water at the base of the canal's crumbling stone wall. It was a firefly, no doubt about it. Where could it possibly have come from, to be flying around this way over foul water that normally carried only night-soil barges?

Ah, the old Edo days! I said to myself, then stopped, feeling utterly foolish. Still, that firefly roaming the air, blinking its little light next to a broken-down wall hundreds of years old, was amazingly cute.